Cherry Single

A Transvestite Comes of Age

Valory Gravois

Alchemist / Light Publishing
Belmont, California

Acknowledgments

Thanks to a teacher who urged a novel and to my spouse, other writers, and transvestites for reading manuscripts and offering suggestions.

Thank God we're not all cut out using the same cookie cutter.

Valory Gravois
Burlingame, California

1

San Francisco, 1971

Keys jangled, quick footsteps thumped down a long stairway and a heavy front door gave way as David Nunley dashed out of his apartment building.

As he aimed himself toward Mission Street, two blocks away, he caught sight of his Muni bus already leaving the stop. He sighed, slowed down, and allowed himself to take in the neighborhood. After an evening rainstorm the air was pungent and crisp, and pastel-hued stucco homes along the way looked fresh and washed in the early morning sunlight. He passed two greasy men trying to jump-start a pickup. Further along, a man throwing the morning's newspapers out of a car narrowly missed him.

Out of the cool air materialized a young, well-dressed Hispanic woman coming up from a side street just ahead. She gave David a quick glance and he returned it before falling in behind her. She was wearing black high heels and the sound of them scratching the sidewalk and echoing from nearby buildings drew his complete attention.

David knew that his nearness bothered her. He could pass her if he wanted, but he slowed so he could dwell on her shoes. At that moment he deliciously remembered that he was wearing panties — and he remembered their slick, shiny material.

He pretended to read a newspaper after they arrived at the bus stop. When the next Muni arrived, he let her get on first and noted where she sat down. As he passed down the isle he was rewarded with a glance down her bodice. The beginnings of two perfect breasts resided there, nestled in a lacy black bra.

Does she know I looked?

Standing in the rear of the bus, he felt the touch of panties against his skin. Who would guess that beneath his plain clothing was such exoticness?

Soon he began looking out the bus's fogged and scratched windows. The motley signs of Mission Street were sliding by — Orozco's Market . . . Dos Amigos Bar . . . the Coronado Theater . . . Rosalie's Wig Shop . . .

Standing there in his wrinkled, long coat, holding the overhead bar, David Nunley looked like a college student. His long, unmanaged hair framed a bemused yet honest face, a cross between young Abraham Lincoln and a Mediterranean-ish male model in *Vogue* or *Bazaar*. When women looked at him, as they often did, he quickly averted his glance.

He was fidgety as he stood, absorbing the lips, earrings, painted fingernails, nylons and dresses around him.

A woman about 10 years older who might have been a secretary or retail clerk was standing next to him. From time to time their bodies touched as the bus lurched down Mission Street. David could have pulled away but didn't, nor did the woman. On this plane of consciousness, he rode the rest of the way downtown.

2

Arriving downtown, David Nunley walked two blocks, then caught an elevator to the fourth floor of a glassed-in high-rise. Exiting the elevator, he passed by a plaque announcing the Western Area Office of the Veterans Administration and entered a cavernous room filled with a labyrinth of cubicles.

The office's mission was the processing of the records and papers the VA used in disbursing its billions in veterans' benefits. David hadn't had much trouble getting the job of correspondence clerk, considering his test scores and veteran's preference. "It's a secure job—the pay's decent," he would reply when asked what he did for a living. As for the women in his department, though, he had to admit that the majority were of the plump, fading and married variety. There were only five single young women in room 420A—and one of them knew more about him than he liked.

A businesslike glance and a good morning from his supervisor greeted David as he walked into his section. Everything about Vince Grasso was brisk. He had the aggressiveness often seen in short men, coupled with a pleasantly ingratiating manner. Vince didn't bother workers who worked reasonably well, reported on time, and seemed busy. He didn't seem to notice when they were typing letters to cousin Joanne or duplicating pornographic cartoons.

It was the second look the supervisor gave David that made him think twice. He felt obligated to return a "Good Morning!" What often bothered David was the fact that Vince was about the same age as himself—twenty-six—yet David felt younger and inferior. Maybe it was the suits Vince wore or the mature cookie-duster mustache he affected.

As David moved down the isle to his cubicle he tried to look at each worker in turn. Some were just settling in at their desks with steaming cups of coffee, including older women with their shapeless dresses and conservative hairdos. Here and there were the men, only one of which David knew well—a young guy called The Jock who followed football.

David passed Corky's cubicle. She evidently hadn't arrived yet. He had expected his heart to leap as he rounded her corner, but there was no Corky. Somehow he couldn't seem to get to work at his desk not having seen her. He looked at the smudgy, obscure Monet print on the wall of his space. He had wanted to replace it with something more exciting but hadn't gotten around to it.

No Corky this morning! David was unsettled. He thought again about the panties he was wearing. His imagination was vivid enough. It took the voice of Mrs. Johnson, the personable black clerk, to dissolve his small arousal with a question about a record he'd handled. She dressed better than most of the women, wore heels and had a contagious smile. After watching her move her sexy hips down the isle, David finally got down to work. His telephone began to ring and his typewriter wrapped him in its arms and lulled him into a work routine.

In the afternoon when he noticed that Corky still wasn't there, he sidled up to Vince. "Where's Corky? Did she call in sick or what?"

His boss looked up from his neat desk with a look of concern. Vince seemed to invest every movement with importance.

"AWOL," he pronounced. "And this is it, Corky's gone too far. I'm getting her canned, fired, whatever you want to call it."

David knew how hard it was to fire someone from a government job, yet Corky had pretty much gone beyond the pale in her flights of freedom. She'd gotten more and more rebellious. David walked back to his desk to face a waiting stack of memos and papers.

After work and a bus ride home, David made his way up the long stairway of his apartment building and opened the leftmost of four identical apartment doors. After having been a poor student rooming with others, David's job had finally allowed him the luxury of his own place.

Inside was a long flat that began with a kitchen, transitioned into a bedroom, and ended in a living room. The apartment was furnished throughout with completely unmatched furniture and thrift store rugs.

David's kitchen was notable for being half a photographic darkroom. A single window had been light-blocked, and yellow-labeled bottles of chemicals shared space with yellow boxes of enlarging paper and stained developing trays. The next room, the bedroom, contained a low Japanese-style dining table surrounded by cushions, with a TV at one end. The bed was simply a mattress and box spring on the floor in one corner, and was never completely made. Stood against a wall was a full-length mirror and an old chest of drawers, with the bottom drawer devoted to women's lingerie and accessories.

Most of David's presence was expressed in the furthermost living room, with its bay windows overlooking a quiet intersection and providing an abundance of daylight.

There were tall bookcases full of photographic books, LP records, and diaries. Pinned on the walls were his own mostly black-and-white photographs of nature, women and political protests. In a place of honor among those was a classy Ansel Adams photo poster of Aspen trees. Scattered about in no particular order were all kinds of photographic gear. Finally, a simple table made from a door supported a typewriter, a serviceable stereo and an aquarium.

On the floor near the bay windows were several flower pots containing eucalyptus trees he'd grown from seed gathered in a nearby park. Without any wind or adversity, they had grown very fast, with very slender stems—just like Ansel Adams' Aspens.

A long hallway offered access to a bathroom and the apartment's only closet, with the extreme left side—out of sight—holding women's things.

In his diaries, David sometimes called this place his ship, where he could be captain, cook, and stowaway woman.

David threw himself and his briefcase on his bed and rested. After dozing briefly, he sat up and looked listlessly out the window. Blank housefronts across the street looked back. He finally stripped down to his panties and searched through his female clothing. Slipping into a lacy white bra and faux breasts, David put his plain white work shirt back on, tucked it into Levi's, and stepped into the living room. He sat down in a plain wooden chair, absentmindedly rubbed his day's beard growth, and thought about calling Corky. When he finally dialed, his heart began to race. He wondered why he had so little control over himself.

Corky's roommate answered. Corky was taking a bath—could she call back? Several hours later, when in the staleness of the evening she still hadn't called, David tried again. Corky came on reluctantly. She had been on her way out the door. "Oh, the job? Tell Vince I think I've quit."

David adopted a somber attitude and reminded her that some people would jump at the chance to have her job.

"I'm really tired of that hole. I can't stand it any more."

"So, what're you going to do now?"

"I suppose I'll get another job. But I'm going to take some time off, a couple weeks. Just float with my friends."

David cringed. Some of her friends scared him. "Well, I'll miss you down there."

"That's the way it is." Then, in a mischievous voice—"Are you wearing panties, Davie?"

"Yes, I am . . ." His voice became squeaky-childlike as though he was in front of a demanding mother. Perversely, there was something thrilling in it all.

"You know, that's how I can handle that office shit. I can come home and wear my goodies." He wished that she was there to share in the wickedness.

After good-byes, he lay back on his carelessly-made bed, closed his eyes and threw one leg over the other. Ah, Corky was becoming so elusive. She really wanted him out of her life.

Lying on his bed, David recalled how she'd moseyed up to him in the office after she'd transferred in from another department. He hadn't liked her much at first. She was short and she seemed cheap and inconsequential.

He remembered her messy desk, her deprecatory remarks about Grasso and the office, her playful, knowing smile and the sexy bras he'd glimpsed beneath her generous necklines. There had been something undernourished about her—a slightly sallow look to her face. On the other hand, she'd always kept her hair nicely done, brassy blonde and very curly. There had been something too about the shape of her pert lips.

He knew it wasn't quite right, but after she asked him casually if he wanted to visit her apartment, one lonely evening he did. They took a marvelously sudsy bath together and later, after some time in bed, he shyly asked if he could wear a pair of her panties. She had played soul music and there were posters of black musicians and actors on the walls.

David lay on his softly lumpy bed and projected the newsreel further. There had been the time when Corky for some mysterious reason—she wouldn't say why—had to vacate her apartment. Could she stay with him? David remembered how bowled over he'd been. He wasn't in love—he'd just never lived with a woman. He remembered how he'd looked forward to just being in the same bed with a woman on a regular basis. He'd never imagined that finding a woman could be so easy.

After she moved in, they would play little touch games at work and go out to lunch together—except for those times when she said she had to meet someone. No, she couldn't say who. Then there were the times when he went off to see a movie by himself in the evening and phoned back to see if everything was OK, just like calling a wife. Corky had seemed bothered.

They had about two good weeks of sex before she began to slip away. David would see her in the office but she spent more and more nights away from the apartment, giving him time to wear her things. Black men dropped her off after midnight. Sometimes he heard them talking at the door before she came in, and one of the men even had the gall to go into the kitchen and have a beer before he left. David had lain riveted to his bed, listening.

Confronted with all this, Corky had merely said, "You and me are just roommates and I'm not making any other promises."

In retaliation David felt less obliged to restrain his dressing when around her. Several nights when she returned to the apartment late she found him partially dressed as a woman, and didn't seem shocked or even embarrassed.

One evening — a rare one — when she was home, David managed to corner her and make her tell about the shadowy part of her life.

"I don't know if you're ready for this. I mean, I wanted to tell you at first but I was afraid you wouldn't want me to stay. You're such a nice guy."

David assured her that he could handle it.

"Well . . . I've been a part-time hooker since even before I met you. So there you have it." She said she'd been hanging around with some guys on the fringes of the music scene and that she did it to get bucks for clothes and partying.

"When you first moved in was I sharing you with a lot of men?"

Corky laughed a little, then threw her head back to gain composure. "Look, you might not believe it, but I was leaving the scene when I left my apartment."

"Then what?"

"Then I met some new dudes — like Maxwell, remember, the guy who came in and got a beer? — who weren't heavy. Pimping was kind of a sport with them. They had money coming in from other places too."

David imagined svelte black men in furs and leathers hunting with falcons.

"So about that time our love life came apart. I had always thought it was because my panties and stuff turned you off."

"Well, David, I've always liked you as a person. But you didn't turn me on too much if you know what I mean. I guess I'm mostly into black guys and discos and all that."

"I'm sorry, but I really keep thinking that my dressing turned you off. I mean, I know that sometimes I look ridiculous."

"It's no big deal—once in awhile a trick is into it. But I don't think you realize how guilty you look when you're wearing women's things. You look like a kid caught jerking off or something."

David looked away.

Resigned to the fact that Corky was lost to the sub-culture, that she'd found her own brand of addiction like his, he'd thought it best to use her in some other way. With her reluctant approval he followed her downtown a half-dozen times and photographed her from a distance as she picked up tricks near Union Square. It was the matter-of-fact way she approached the whole thing, the way she dressed to provoke men, that interested him. Also, there was the challenge of operating stealthily to avoid an incident with a customer.

It began to bother him more and more that he'd failed with her. She'd become a sex goddess and he just another john. The few times he still found her back at the apartment he peppered her with questions— "How could I turn you on? . . . Why do you like black men more than me?"

He had finally reached the hazy conclusion that he should see other women.

David snapped back to the reality of his bedroom and listened to rain hitting his darkened window. The clear, strong, wet darkness on the other side of the pane seemed refreshing. Inside, though, his weak room-light cast a yellowish pall over everything. He closed his eyes to this and began to fantasize. He thought of playing a game with Corky where she would pick him up off the street. As they entered her hotel room, she would know exactly what to do. She would make him disrobe and tie him down to a bed with black leather thongs. Then she'd wrap a thin whip around his penis and pull on it.

David's hand work eventually brought him to a strong orgasm and he lay for a few seconds with sperm resting in his palm. He basked in the contentment and warmth of his body for long minutes, then held up his sperm. For a moment it seemed to have religious significance—after all, there was the feeling that he had leaped aboard something greater than himself. Then the sperm began to look slightly repulsive. He was so evil now and he was all alone like a little boy in the middle of a dark gymnasium. He took off his bra and panties and slowly, creaking at the joints, got up to straighten things and make himself a late evening snack.

Munching on his cheese-melts, he walked over to look at his favorite photo of Corky, a blow-up of her wearing pin curlers and a sexy push-up bra. He'd shot it through one of her nylons, giving the photo a soft glow.

Now she was pushing him away after he'd asked her to move. There had been too many men dropping her off who might have ripped off his camera equipment and too many times when she went AWOL for days at a stretch, calling in sick to work and later telling him, "Oh, I was in LA!" She had finally moved in with a woman roommate somewhere across the Bay without giving him her address.

Perhaps the only lasting negative fallout had been when he wrote his parents in Ohio about his living with a woman. Not unexpectedly, a damning letter arrived from his father and a softer-toned letter from his mother. His father's choice of words was unfortunate. David had become angry himself, so angry that he'd replied, "There is the fact that I'm much worse a boy than you imagine. I dress up as a woman whenever I can."

David turned on his dusty and scratched TV. He felt both very free and very lonely. After watching nothing memorable for an hour he put on a nightgown and went to sleep. Halfway through the night when the slippery material began to ride up around his waist, he took it off and pushed it off onto the floor.

3

David hardly ever thought about his parents back in Ohio. In fact, he was relieved that the whole shocking mess was finally out in the open because it distanced them even further. He knew how his father took the revelation—his father who'd always hated effeminate men and thought they were homos.

Corky continued to preoccupy David. She was on his mind as he worked, usually seeming alluring, cheap and heavenly, all at the same time. Walking the streets, he kept thinking that he saw her in buses or cars, staring at him impassively.

He managed to see her once more when he offered to take her out to a fancy downtown restaurant. She was wearing an expensive new leather jacket.

"What did you discover about me when you lived with me?" he asked earnestly, yet with a small smile about his lips. He didn't want to seem too involved—this was only an intellectual curiosity. "Really, Corky, don't be afraid of hurting me, just tell the truth. My dressing turned you off, didn't it?"

If she made any new answers he couldn't remember them afterward. It was as though his questions themselves were an attempt at sex. She did say that she was working at a small shop in Ghirardelli Square and implied that it had become a wonderful way to meet horny men with money to burn. The owner of the store was naive and "maybe" she was draining a few bucks. Yes, she was still with her black friends and there'd been a couple scrapes with the law. David figured she'd end up in jail somewhere even though she always bragged about knowing cops.

He asked if he could take a picture of her before they parted. "You take too many pictures," she replied. "I want you to send all your pictures of me. You know, legally they're mine. You can't do anything with them."

"Bullshit. They're mine." His anger surprised him.

"You try to show them or sell them anywhere and I'll take you to court."

He wanted to slap her a wide swath with his hand as he'd seen in the movies but instead walked out of the restaurant behind her, invisibly getting his camera ready. When they reached the sidewalk he brought the Minolta up quickly. The compact hunk of glass and steel made a loud click and Corky kicked out at him. He walked away quickly before she could draw a crowd.

When he developed and printed the photo later he thought he'd captured her essential stoniness — pursed lips and unfeeling, angry eyes. Now, looking at it, he could masturbate even more, dwelling on how she would want to hurt him and how she would enjoy it all.

Eventually a new person was brought in to take over Corky's desk in room 420A. The new clerk was Eugene J. Gatzo, a transfer from the Phoenix office. Gene was an occasional stutterer who looked rather earnest and efficient with a big, rounded forehead and trim mustache. Enhancing those effects were his thick eyeglasses.

Gene seemed bright enough in the few contacts David had with him, even perhaps ambitious — the kind of guy who might take the silly job seriously. However, David soon noticed that Gene had the annoying tendency to launch himself indiscriminately into every knot of people in the office. He was soon avoided by most and by women especially.

Salacious or racial jokes usually good for a laugh in mixed company instantly became offensive when given the Gatzo touch. He seemed to have the straight-backed bearing of a military man without any suaveness.

Then there was that stutter.

Those very qualities, though, intrigued David. He decided to go to lunch with the newcomer half out of curiosity, half as a favor. They headed for a popular Chinese cafeteria on Beale Street. As usual, it was packed.

Gene stood in the food line ramrod straight and ordered the healthy items. After they lucked out and found a table next to the front window, David complimented his choices.

"Thank you, thank you," Gatzo said with a quick, self-satisfied smile. There was something in Gene's voice that reminded David of the silly chipmunk records of the 50s and 60s. "I've really learned a lot the last couple of years. I s-suppose you could say that I've got the health bug. Been reading books on nutrition and vitamins. It's been helping me. I feel really a-alert and balanced."

David nodded affirmatively and wondered where Gene had picked up "balanced."

"Have you read Adelle Davis?" asked Gene.

David nodded. It was too bad about Gatzo. Maybe he, David, could help him somehow. Maybe he could give him a few social pointers. Meanwhile, a woman walked by outside and David turned to see if she was Corky.

Gene was going on about various other disciplines he'd been involved in — karate, intensive journal, EST, self-hypnosis and transactional analysis. That last term caught David's ear. He'd heard it mentioned before, maybe in the newspaper, but he didn't know much about it. Gene rattled on that he'd started visiting a transactional analyst in San Francisco after having been with one in Phoenix.

David asked Gene why he'd moved. Gene muttered, "I-I guess I wanted to be by myself. I was kind of under my parents' thumb in Phoenix — didn't feel like I had any freedom. I mean, I don't want you to get the wrong idea — they're nice people."

"They jumped in whenever you gave them an opening?"

"More or less," he said as he took off his heavy glasses, disclosing eyes that were surprisingly tender and liquid. He carefully wiped the lenses as though massaging a part of himself, then put the glasses back on and looked around the cafeteria. David did too and wondered what the other well-dressed people were talking about — surely not about relationships with parents. David realized that he'd talked about his parents with so many girlfriends over the years, especially when he was into Freud, that he'd exhausted the subject.

Gene continued. "My family is so s-s-success oriented. My parents made a lot of money in real estate. My sister has a Ph.D. and teaches out East. One brother is a major in the Army and the other is assistant manager at an auto dealership. Then there's little old me. My folks put me through an expensive college to become a VA clerk?" Gene's hand was shaking slightly.

"Sounds a little like me," said David, laughing.

"We h-had some arguments. I knew I had to get out of there."

"How old are you?"

"Twenty-six."

"Say, how do the women out here compare with back there?" David coaxed. "I'm assuming you're not married."

"Really, you've got some fabulous women around here. I mean, they dress to kill. I've been trying to meet a few."

David winced at a fleeting memory of Corky. "How's it been going?"

Gene took a deep breath before answering. "Oh, I've been turned down a couple times. B-But it's probably just a matter of time."

On the walk back to the VA building, David had Gene tell him more about transactional analysis, or, as Gene called it, TA. There was something about the word *transactional* that attracted David. Gene was saying something about the various mental states — child . . . adult . . . and parent. TA was supposed to be a more efficient approach to mental health than psychoanalysis. David, allowing a little proselytizing, promised to go out and buy a book about it. As they went to their separate cubicles in room 420A, David felt more comfortable with Gene Gatzo.

David needed to dress more after Corky left, but he wasn't making enough money to seriously indulge his desires. Also there was the matter of his embarrassment at going to Macy's or the Emporium to shop. Someone he knew might spot him looking at pantyhose. He was never sure whether the sales clerks guessed or not.

He bought several new wigs and a long corset from Fredericks by mail, wondering if the mailman had put two and two together. On weekends he took pictures of himself in various stages of dress and developed and printed them. There were explosive masturbations after he had paraded in front of the mirror and camera, becoming different personalities as he changed his costumes. If a neighbor knocked on his door he had to become totally silent and wait for the person to go away. At the end of a session his bedroom and living room would be littered with clothing, false breasts, lingerie and camera equipment. Then he would get mildly depressed and go grocery shopping just to get out and be around people.

At the same time, he wrote long entries in his diary about his ecstasies, along with half-amused soliloquies such as "I know I'm a very evil person" and "I am so, so sinful." He solemnly wrote that he needed to go out and meet women. "But how? At the laundromat, the supermarket? On the bus?" He wished he wasn't so shy and unconfident.

Several years previously in his diary he'd spent much time and many pages trying to jot down his formative childhood before it trickled out of memory. The mere act of writing seemed to make him feel better, like talking to an all-accepting listener.

He recorded his early visions of having his penis cut or sawed, and the vivid daydreams of his father looming over him intoning hatefully while everything seemed to grow menacingly large.

"Everything my father wasn't, my mother was," David wrote. "She was the delicate, understanding person I sided with early on, especially when she and dad argued. She was soft and pretty while he was a wall of granite."

Where in his childhood David had experienced his first heartthrob over his mother's undergarments he couldn't remember. He remembered wearing her tight swimsuit and old-fashioned girdles, and her soft sweaters and dresses. His inclination was to write on and on and speculate endlessly but too much writing made him ill. He would become too buried in the past and feel out of control. David had never shown the diaries to anyone, having hidden them from Corky because she never admitted to having dreams and fantasies anyway.

David was keenly feeling that it was time to understand his dressing further. Maybe transactional analysis was the answer, even as loath as he was to trust in a group activity.

4

Feeling debauched after one of his weekends of play, David arrived at the office on a Monday needing regimen and regular people to straighten him out. Gene Gatzo was at work early as usual, almost as early as the boss.

Gene approached and asked if he had enjoyed his days off.

"It was pretty quiet. Had some letter-writing to do. Hiked around a little," David fabricated.

Gene brightened. "H-Hiking's-s something I used to do a lot of. Where'd you go?"

David was both annoyed and sorry for Gene. Annoyed because he, David, had to listen harder and suppress a superior smile at the labored speech, and sorry because Gene was embarrassed when he stuttered.

"I like to hike up around Muir Woods, Mount Tam and all that. One problem is that I don't have a car."

He hadn't counted on Gene having one. The new clerk asked through his thick glasses if David would like to trek over to one of those places on the next weekend. With reservations and an attitude of we'll-try-it-once, David agreed. He put on a smile for Gene as they parted. In fact, the smile wasn't *all* false.

The hike went better than David expected. Gene's stutter almost disappeared and there was a certain buddy-buddyness in walking side by side along the roads and trails of the Point Reyes area.

Fog persisted most of the day and the pair passed wet berry bushes set between plain, high, rounded hills. At one point they encountered a gray ocean surf coming out of the mists which David photographed in every possible way.

In casual clothes and with knapsack Gene looked more human. He was shorter than David and seemed like a younger brother. Their talk meandered, with Gene saying that he'd stuttered from pre-teen days and that he'd tried almost everything to lose it. David mentioned a time in high school when he was talking to a stutterer and found himself unintentionally imitating the fellow. The stutterer, thinking he was the object of a joke, threatened to hit him. The story made Gene genuinely laugh for the first time.

They'd had some of the same experiences—trying out for sports in high school without much success, hitches in the military, and an early love for science fiction. Eventually the talk got around to women. Gene was saying in a sudden pique, "Women. How the h-hell do you meet them around here anyway? I've been going to this country bar in Albany—and so far the only lady I've gotten interested in me was 55 and drunk."

David laughed. "Maybe you ought to check out some other places. You live in San Francisco, right? It's a mecca for women. You mean to tell me you can't find any women here?"

"Where should I go? I mean, you've been around here a lot longer than me."

"You just need to circulate. Go out and do things you feel like doing. Take classes that women go to. Join the Sierra Club and go on group hikes." David realized he should be following his own advice.

"One thing I did—I saw fliers about a group called Ron Johnston's Saturday Night Experience. It's this guy who teaches seminars on how to meet people. You know, ten steps to meeting a woman and getting a date. Then Ron and his partner have parties on Saturday nights for meeting people. I went to the class — cost me $50 — then to the party. Thirty eligible men, three foxy ladies and a dozen old maids."

"So, which one of the foxy ladies did you get?" kidded David. "But seriously, maybe you shouldn't try to start at the top of the heap. Just go out with *someone*."

"Yeah, maybe so," allowed Gene, looking down absent-mindedly and digging his toe into soft, moist earth. "I'll bet you have a lot of girlfriends, huh?" He had heard about Corky.

"Put that in the past tense." David went on to describe in a censored version his disappointment with Corky.

"But look at you, David," said the little hiker, "you're what the girls all want — tall, handsome — "

David pictured himself with a bra on his hairy chest.

"intelligent . . ."

"All of those things, naturally," quipped David. He lectured lightly on how personality and soul counted the most.

"But you have to get in the front door," insisted Gene.

"Just pull down her zipper. Just kidding. Really, don't worry so much. With all the gay men around there's tons of extra women to choose from."

Gene wanted to know how David's camera worked, and their hands touched while fiddling with the controls. David said he'd give some instruction if Gene ever bought a decent SLR. Then he regretted his promise. Maybe Gene would get too attached to him. He didn't want any funny stuff happening.

While riding back home David probed Gene for more information about transactional analysis. He had always shied away from EST and Esalen and their devotees but he decided to look at TA. Later, Gene lent him his introductory paperback *I'm OK, You're OK*. Also, Gene had mentioned how he liked his TA analyst, a Mrs. Osaki. David cautioned himself that Gene was the kind of guy who might exaggerate things but maybe he would check out this Asian woman. He would do it without telling Gene, though. Gene didn't need to know that he wanted to see anyone. He started to read the paperback with its yellow-highlighted passages.

David ended up consuming three TA books. He remembered that he'd read *Games People Play* some time before without connecting it to a therapy, but he skimmed it again anyway. Then it was *I'm OK, You're OK* and finally *What Do You Say After You Say Hello?* He read the three at about the same speed he'd read a novel.

Finally David worked up the courage to call Dr. Osaki's office.

At the appointed time one evening David arrived at an imposing, tree-shrouded house in the middle- to upper-middle class Richmond District after walking three misty blocks from a bus stop. He double-checked the house number and found an embossed business card thumbtacked to the heavy wooden door —

Maria Ollswell Osaki, Ph.D.
Transactional Analyst
A.T.A.A., A.P.S.

David rang the doorbell. What sort of venomous man-eating creatures would be inside to dissect him? Or would there be some lithesome, beautiful lady-creatures to tell him how unique, brilliant and attractive he was?

Finally the door opened and he was invited into a crowded, warm interior. The rooms were quite comfortable, with dark-hued wood paneling, ancient floor lamps, ferns, muted Oriental rugs and glistening hardwood floors. The house was the sort where murder mysteries are filmed, with secret sliding panels.

David stood in the front room taking in all of this as the host went to find a chair. He made an effort to look at the others in the room. There were several men like himself, painfully quiet. To David the women seemed at ease and talkative while the men were rough-edged and quirky.

David asked a woman if Mrs. Osaki was there.

"She's not here yet. She's usually late, anyway — a very busy lady, you know."

David nodded and began looking at faces again. But the woman, who said she'd been in the program for three months, continued talking endlessly about Osaki's abilities. David was irritated, yet figured that being seen talking with this woman would make him appear more sociable. Finally the woman excused herself. David grabbed a magazine, and, while pretending to read, imagined telling a fictional Maria Osaki that he was a transvestite. She would have the others grab him and hold him down while she would hold lingerie against his genitals and give him an embarrassing erection.

Maria Ollswell Osaki hustled in a half-hour late with looseleaf binders, books, a strong leather briefcase and an air of take-charge. But rather than the spare, Japanese woman with chopsticks in her belt that David expected, the overweight fiftyish Caucasian woman came in wearing bright and discordant polyester. David told himself that he didn't need to return after this first gratuitous meeting.

Mrs. Osaki, matronly and dignified facially, spoke in a no-nonsense way and was accorded an obvious respect. She began by asking a woman and her lover when they would pay their account. Working that out, Maria, as she was called by the regulars, greeted David and another newcomer.

The session began with the kind of bloodletting David had seen at a past encounter group. There was an alcoholic, a violently jealous lover and a man who couldn't offer affection to his wife. A man who seemed gay told intimate things about himself but never mentioned his sexual inclination. The words *child, adult, parent, permission* and *script* were often used by Mrs. Osaki. David remained silent and watched the people around him reveal themselves. He sat poised on his chair as though ready to spring into the air at the first opportunity to confess his sins.

All through the session the eminently practical Osaki kept the discussion relevant. She was a woman of some experience. Her favorite comment was "That's bullshit." She came on like a Jewish mother and never failed to make fun of those who took themselves too seriously. Still, David harbored doubts about her.

At the end of the meeting the atmosphere quickly changed. Those souls who'd seemed so wounded and over the edge appeared to heal themselves instantly. The conversation went back to jobs and "How are you and Chris doing?"

David was given a ride home by the other new person, a comely woman who also couldn't say enough good things about

Dr. Osaki. He gave her a peck on the cheek as a good-by then went up into his apartment and straight to bed. New people, new thoughts and new feelings rattled his brain. Alone again and master of his space, he quickly drifted off to sleep.

5

The following weekend David walked into the offices of *The Real Times*. Residing in a sway-backed storefront in the industrial South-of-Market district, the *Times* was one of the surviving underground newspapers from the 1960s. The Corky thing had taken him out of contact with the paper and he wanted to touch base again.

The day before, President Nixon had begun the bombing of Hanoi. David had read every newspaper account. Some aspects of war excited him but not this impersonal rain of destruction. The Russians claimed bomb damage to one of their cargo ships; the Vietnamese, to a hospital. This expansion of the Viet Nam war also made David aware of the probability of more anti-war demonstrations in San Francisco.

As he expected, there was just a skeleton crew working in the newspaper office, since an issue of the weekly had just hit the newsstands. When one of the hippie girls running the front desk —what was her name, Starr?—greeted him by name, he knew they hadn't forgotten him. He heard another woman taking down a sex ad from the phone. As it happened, the newspaper's financial underpinning was massage parlor and sexual classified ads — the *Times* would print any ad short of solicitations for child porn and snuff movies.

The inside of the storefront was wallpapered with posters of rock musicians, posters of pigs dressed in cops' uniforms, and photos of brutal riot police at San Francisco State and People's Park. In fact, David's first association with the paper had been during those incidents. One of his photos, which he could claim had been on the cover of the publication, was still on the wall — a black-and-white of an attractive woman wearing only a skimpy bra, panties and a big smile being escorted by two male gas-masked students, fully clothed. The *Times* was just that — a mix of fun and seriousness, blood and music, pubescent rebellion and reverence.

Don Hill, the acting editor in lieu of the ailing owner, was sitting at his messy roll-top desk talking to the ad manager, whose bushy hairdo attained such an extraordinary volume that birds might have nested in it. Both were reviewing the just-released issue.

Finally Don was free and David meandered over, shyly walking between art layout tables where several long-haired workers were beginning to create ad pages for the next issue. Don was a thin, bespectacled man with short hair who carried a certain air of authority and caring. His worn corduroy sports jacket was a trademark. David asked what was happening politically.

"Big demonstration Monday," said Don. "Civic Center downtown. Everyone's pretty pissed about how desperate Kissinger and Nixon have gotten."

"Well, I'd like to cover it," offered David, knowing he'd have to call in sick to attend the affair. "Who else'll be there?"

Don named the staff photographer, a writer-photographer couple and "Oh yes, a photographer named Diane Beckel-something who came in a few days ago from the East Coast."

A surge of resentment rose in David. Competing with the staff photographer for picture space was bad enough, but to have to compete against the young upstarts . . . Oh well, she'd probably turn in lousy prints and they'd kiss her off.

"Then it's OK if I cover the Monday thing?"

Don indicated that he could cover whatever he wanted. "Get some good cop shots—you know, snouts, piggy tails, et cetera. And take care—we don't need any more hospital cases or cracked skulls." They shook hands and parted.

David wandered over to a vacant desk to finish reading the just-released issue. As he read he remembered how the newspaper had contributed to the breakdown with his parents. He had once innocently sent them a copy. They said they'd burned it after seeing only the cover, which to David had been innocuous. Well, there had been some pubic hair showing.

In the latest issue there was an article about the Cockettes, the outlandish and irrepressible female impersonator troupe, and about sexual identity liberation. David reflected that he'd never told anyone at the *Times* about being a transvestite. Women would come to the *Times* office wearing men's shirts and trousers and some of the men wore rather flowing garments and earrings. But David tended to dress in a decidedly male fashion, often wearing an army fatigue jacket over Levi's.

Maybe it was because of his secrets that he sometimes felt he was a spy when he visited the *Times*. Once a staffer asked him point-blank if he worked for the pigs. Other workers came under suspicion too, but David down deep felt like an infiltrator and impostor. Even in his dreams, he often played that role.

When he finished skimming the *Times'* news stories and photos and was sure that no one was looking, he skipped to the back of the newspaper to the sex ads. In a section titled *Further Out*, he found —

> *Mistress Leeta knows your secret desires and shows no mercy. Get on your knees and lick my boots. 559-7708.*

Workers in the newspaper office snickered about these. David had never worked up the courage to answer one. Maybe he would, he thought, some time when he could afford to—or if the urgency could let him wait no longer.

David returned home. Sunlight streamed in through the bay windows and the day was warming up unusually for an early spring Saturday. He spent some time straightening up his apartment, throwing away accumulated magazines and newspapers, and washing two days of dishes in the kitchen-darkroom.

The doldrums of the weekend stretched before him. He wanted to go out and hike or bicycle but he pictured himself doing those things feeling lonely and isolated. He could go see a movie but would it turn out to be a good one? It might be one that left him bored, with a headache and time lost. Here he was alone again. There were women he could call but none had seemed especially interested in him. He didn't like to beg.

He began to imagine dressing as a woman, putting lingerie and silky fabrics on his body and feeling sexy. He wanted to dress well enough to look in the mirror and say, "This is how it feels to be a woman." He thought he needed some new garments, not the tired old things in his closet and drawers. His paycheck from the day before would make a shopping trip possible.

He remembered a certain corset shop on Mission Street that had tempted him many times. He made his way out of the apartment into the fresh, sunny air. Taking a crowded bus, he summoned enough courage to get off at 22nd and Mission in the heart of the Hispanic district. There could be no hesitation, no turning back. Through crowds of shoppers, he walked up to Alana's Corset Shop trying to seem at ease, stopping briefly at the display window to admire clear plastic torsos with perfectly-filled bras and corsets.

David joined a stout Mexican-American woman being served at the counter. Two teenage girls were fingering filmy panties on a rack. Eventually the saleswoman got around to asking if he needed help.

"Yeah, ah . . . I'd like to buy some lingerie for my wife."

"Yes, yes, sir," said the señora. "And what do you look for?"

"I think a bra," said David. "Maybe a corset." He began to sweat when he heard the girls giggle. The proprietor brought out two dainty white corsets. He looked at the price tags and managed a little laugh. "I think I'd better look at bras instead."

"What size, sir?" The woman impatiently looked off to one side.

David fumbled with a slip of paper he took from his pocket. "Ah, a 38B." As the saleslady went to get some bras, he remembered the time he and Corky had gone shopping together—he'd shyly handed her money and told her which lingerie to buy. She'd gleefully embarrassed him at Penny's by holding a bra up against his chest.

David left the shop carrying a lacy black bra with slender straps. He recalled how the saleswoman had handled the bra sexily, running her fingers along the inside of the cups as though to seduce him.

His compulsiveness was an overly-ripe fruit as he boldly made his way through other stores buying a new half-slip, a dress, and a long wig. At the women's shoe store he had a hard time because of his man-sized feet. Only through trial and error in the past had he learned what size fit him. He had to settle for a rather commonplace pair.

When the VA clerk got on the bus with his packages, with his checking account nearly exhausted, he felt excited, magic and guilty all at once. *Some men hire prostitutes, but I am my own prostitute.*

Guarding his packages in his lap, he mused about the early days when he accumulated things by stealing from his mother. Then there were the several times he thought that dressing was ruining his manhood and burned his stash.

Arriving home after the bus had labored up his small hill, he excitedly spread out the day's purchases on his bed. In the messy apartment they seemed perfect and right, with price tags still on them and the elastic stiff and new. The wig was fragrant as though from a real woman.

David went into the bathroom to pin his long hair back and to shave as closely as possible. As usual when he was in a hurry he made a small cut on his Adam's apple. The little stainless steel shelf beneath the bathroom mirror was soon full of cosmetics. David applied a grease stick over his beard trace to hide it, remembering the time when he was in a grade school play and his mother had put lipstick on him—ick! And how those very same foreign, alien things in stylish containers now captivated him. Men's toiletries came in dull, square bottles with thick wooden stoppers.

He worked with eyeliner, mascara and eye shadow. Lipstick. Rouge. The silence in the bathroom was total. He wasn't aware of the other tenants moving about their apartments or the street sounds outside. What he was doing was injecting a steady stream of excitement into his veins.

The sun shone into the all-white bathroom. He momentarily reflected that anyone on the fire escape outside the window or on the roof of the ramshackle shed across the street might see him primping. It was dangerous being a pervert.

On the matter of perversion, he had been quite along in years before he even knew his quirk had a name, or that he shared it with anyone. Where had it been—in one of Freud's books?—that he had unearthed the word *trans-ves-tite*, even more momentous a discovery than finding *ho-mo-sex-ual* in *Reader's Digest.*

After putting the finishing touches on his facial artwork, David framed it with the new, perfect wig. His heart rose as he admired his perfect woman's face in the mirror. He felt the caress of panty hose and the new slip, and the pressing in of the new brassiere's straps across his back. A padded girdle was authoritatively tight around his middle and genitals. He turned himself in front of the bathroom mirror and posed in various angles so he could see his breasts and hair.

Suddenly there was a shout. He dove below the level of the second-story window and waited with heart racing, feeling like some female soldier in war. Finally, peeking, he saw a man with a beer belly loading the trunk of a large American car down on the street. Whoever it was couldn't see him.

David slipped away to his bedroom to try on his new heels and dress and admire himself in the full-length mirror. He practiced walking in the unsure footing of the heels for a time, slowly, until he finally approached the mirror. Like a teenage girl practicing provocative moves, he angled his head just right, pushed a wisp of hair this way and that, and pursed his lips. Eventually he drew closer and closer to the mirror until he kissed the approaching woman in the glass. The surface was cold.

He set up a camera to photograph himself, thinking that if only he had a car and it was nighttime he could drive around to see if men would look at him. He felt as potent as a loaded pistol—as Marilyn as Marilyn Monroe, as Sophia as Sophia Loren. After taking many pictures of himself, holding his sexual excitement at bay, he sat down and typed an entry for his diary. Pleasurably, he pushed aside strands of long hair from his eyes. He called himself Natalie.

I'm sitting up here in my ship, fully dressed. Someone might be able to see me, maybe. What a contrast — my clean and nicely-colored dress, my perfect face and hair, and the dirty windows and run-down buildings across the street. I feel fulfilled and sexy, yet everything around me is decaying. Natalie is my friend, always there when I need her. Thank God I have this apartment all to myself.

Natalie lay down on her bed and relaxed. She slowly, teasingly, reached down and pulled her girdle and nylons away so as to touch her penis. She imagined making love to someone else and alternately that someone was making love to her.

When David called in ill Monday morning Vince was skeptical but finally OK'd sick leave. Hoping that no one from the VA office was attending the midday demonstration, David dressed in his photographer's uniform, a long, tropical fatigue shirt he'd brought back from 'Nam that provided multiple pockets for photo paraphernalia. Rolls of film in the pockets felt like bullets — or breasts — bobbing around as he walked. He worried that lingering traces of mascara or nail polish might give his weekend excesses away.

As he walked toward San Francisco's Civic Center plaza from the bus stop he hoped that the demonstration would turn wild — that people would be upset enough over the bombings of Hanoi and Haiphong to raise some hell. The hotter the action the better the pictures he got.

Protesters were forming up in front of City Hall, waiting for formalities to begin. It always helped to have an imposing concrete manifestation of government as a backdrop. David's excitement rose as he stepped closer. Old men sitting on park benches were muttering and leaving, replaced by longhairs and shorter-haired communists, by Maoists and serious activists, and by families with kids in strollers. David began photographing these types as they stood or sat waiting. Several objected, suggesting obliquely that he worked for the police. David hoped that mentioning the *Times* would smooth things out but it failed to impress. Even the *Times* was suspect these days, and many women had an intense dislike of the weekly's sex ads. It would help, David thought, if he had a beard and wore a beret with a red star—Fidel Castro drag.

David looked at the other photographers, some of whom were familiar from past demonstrations, and wondered if his new competition, Diane-somebody, was there.

Several activists asked him to join the demonstration. He winced—they were always trying to get him to commit himself. David had long thought that demonstrations were silly but had never dared say that to their faces. He was there only to record the event.

After the last speech, which had been interrupted repeatedly by Maoists, a coalition leader jumped to the stage, grabbed the microphone and yelled, "Let's stop talking and start taking some righteous action! We're marching to the old Federal Building, the building the killer military recruiters work out of. We're not going to let anyone in so long as Nixon keeps bombing North Viet Nam. Come on now, let's let 'em know we're comin'!"

David scurried along with other photographers to be in front of the marching throng that formed. A long banner unfurled by the foremost proclaimed "Victory To The Viet Cong And All Oppressed Peoples" while the crowd chanted "Ho, Ho, Ho Chi Minh—Ho, Ho, Ho Chi Minh." They're like schoolkids at a pep rally, David thought as they headed toward the other end of the plaza.

Soon a moving line formed around the long granite building which occupied a small city block. Throngs of protesters parked themselves in front of doors. David joined the moving line for a time, wanting to be in the center of things to spot picture possibilities. Thinking that some shaggy demonstrator or paranoiac would come up and accuse him of working for the police, he bought a Nixon button with the "x" cleverly replaced by a swastika.

The city fathers responded slowly but deliberately. San Francisco police, outfitted with riot helmets and head-knocking sticks, marched in and stood in formation opposite the main door. Between them and the door formed a large clot of intent

young men and women who began to sing protest songs in earnest. David put a short telephoto lens on his camera and began
zeroing in on the cops as pent-up violence and anger permeated
the air.

The demonstrators, appealing to a divine right to block
doors, even after orders to disperse from a police lieutenant, were
shocked and outraged when the police struck. The first sounds of
clubs contacting flesh and bone punctuated by shrieks reached
David's ears. Instantly, adrenaline spurted into his veins.
Breathing excitedly and making sure he stayed out of the cops'
range, David began getting good shots. He photographed a hap-
less bystander, a thin fellow holding a bicycle, being set upon by
four predatory riot police. In the space of three minutes it was all
over. There were bloody heads, hands trussed behind backs —
rather sexual, thought David — and more shouting.

Later someone set a Navy recruiter's car on fire but the cops
let it burn out by itself. As David photographed his version of the
scarred hulk, a smiling young woman with two taped and battered Nikon cameras around her neck approached him. She had a
well-defined, tanned face and wore a quilted vest over a plaid
shirt with sleeves rolled up. Her long, dark brown hair, parted in
the middle, was secured in back by an ornately carved barrette,
and her tight Levi's were of the properly faded variety. She asked
if he was David Nunley.

"That would be me." David studied her mischievous brown
eyes and busy, slender lips.

"The people over at the *Times* office said I might run into
you here. I'm Diane Beckelmeyer."

"Oh yeah, they told me about you." He liked that name,
Beckelmeyer. It sounded like a German bakery. "Where are you
in from? They said some place out East."

"Lately from Philadelphia. I was with *Streets* there."

Streets was a well-known alternative paper. David returned
to studying her face and forgot to make conversation. "Ah —" she
continued, "how was your shooting?"

"Never know 'til I see it. Oh, I'm sure I got a couple nice
ones."

"You were close to that one poor guy getting clubbed by all
those fucking pigs." She looked off to the side from time to time
as if looking for more picture opportunities.

"Should have some g-g-great close-ups of that." *I never stutter!* "What do you plan to do out here? Are you making it on photography or what?"

"Oh, kind of hand-to-mouth, you know. I've got my kid, Bobby, with me. We're staying with a friend in the Haight."

David wondered who the friend was.

"The reason I wanted to locate you was 'cause I don't have a darkroom yet and I'm trying to find someone to develop my film."

"I usually don't do stuff for other people—I've got this regular full-time job. But hey, today's different. I took the day off and was going to do darkroom right away. So if you'd like to come over we could develop all of our film."

"Jeez, I have to go back and take care of my son. If you're going to run your darkroom, could you develop and contact print for me? There's a free dinner in it for you sometime—and I could make it over tonight to see how it came out."

He took her film, warm with body heat, provided his phone number and address, and watched her leave across the plaza, walking buoyantly in the direction of Market Street. Old men were reclaiming their benches and a few indigenous crazies were returning to scare tourists. Just as David was stealing a telephoto shot of her, she looked back over her shoulder and waved. At the same time a great mass of fluttering pigeons flew between them. He took that to be a good omen.

6

As usual, he was slower developing film than he'd planned. When Diane Beckelmeyer arrived at seven, dressed more femininely than before, he was in the middle of developing the final rolls of film. Being used to performing his developing ritual alone, he apologized for being preoccupied.

"No problem," said Diane. "I just want to know how my negs came out." She smelled fresh and seemed perky to David, sluggish after watching the darkroom clock for several hours. Her body lightly touched his as he held up a strip of negatives to the ceiling light and they scanned the transparent frames. It was her film, not as evenly exposed as David liked, but there seemed to be a fair number of printable pictures on it. She seemed to like close-ups of faces.

He hung that roll of film in the drying cabinet, handling the wet strip delicately. "I can hardly wait for the contact print of that," she said. As he brought her back a beer from the refrigerator he could see the thin straps of her brassiere through the back of her soft sweater.

The next roll was David's and they made to look at that one together. To his instant horror, some of the pictures he'd taken of himself in drag were on the roll along with shots from the demonstration. His face heated to fever pitch and he made abruptly to put the roll in the drying cabinet. Diane casually stopped him and asked, "Who's this?" — pointing to a negative of himself hiking up his dress to reveal a garter belt and nylons. Other nearby frames were equally incriminating.

He frantically hoped that she couldn't make out his features beneath the wig. "A friend. You know, a friend? As you might suspect, I didn't intend for you to see these." He made a nervous laugh.

"My, my, a very sexy friend." Diane smiled knowingly.

"Oh, we did it for fun. I'm not your cold-ass pornographer." He managed to change the subject.

After the contact printing, with the prints hung up to dry, David showed her around his rooms. Just as he began to worry about having to make a play for her, she said she hadn't eaten dinner yet—had he? David had, but said no. Could he make something?

"Is there a Chinese restaurant around here?"

He told her about Yee's, two blocks down Mission Street. But she picked a different place on the way, the corner burger joint he'd always avoided. As they entered, teenagers and loud music jarred his senses. Diane happily settled into a booth and said the place reminded her of Philly.

"Do you come in here much?" she asked.

"Once in a while," he lied, squirming in his seat.

"Kids," said Diane, "that's where the real action is. I was photographing them back home."

"Why'd you leave?"

"Divorce. Technically, separation. Wanted to get away from the scene of the crime, so to speak." She laughed engagingly. "Go to the land of golden opportunity." Her husband had been an assistant professor who'd dropped out in the sixties to try a variety of middling jobs without success. She, on the other hand, was making a go of photography. Finally she had left with her son.

David depreciated his possibilities as they sat eating deluxe burgers and shakes. They were alike only in that they were on the fringes of the underground newspaper scene. Still, he was drawn to her vitality and directness and realized that he was chasing her, that he wanted something in her.

He tried to suppress an involuntary yawn but she noticed and suggested they part company for the evening. "Do you want your negatives and stuff?" he asked, irked. "You do want to get some prints in to the *Times*, don't you?"

They returned to the apartment, where she chose several shots for him to blow up. Afterwards, he walked her down to her vehicle, a venerable Land Rover, and squeezed her hand as a good-by. Then they both kissed lightly. Her lips seemed cool and warm, soft and sure, all at the same time.

The next morning David was ten minutes late to work, with several excuses on tap. Vince glanced up at him, asking if he felt okay.

David found a staggering accumulation of files on his desk. He fantasized taking half the dull-brown folders and soundlessly putting them back on Grasso's desk. That would show him. David wondered why he was getting this treatment, as though Vince had evidence he hadn't been sick. Maybe one of the other clerks had told on him. The tough part was that he had been in such a good mood before he arrived at his desk. The day of violence had made him feel alive again. That and the captivating Diane Beckelmeyer. Beckelmeyer would forever be a sexy name for him.

He told himself it wouldn't do any good to protest. He would just work at his usual slow speed and not be pressured. He tried to breathe slowly through his nose to calm himself, as he'd read how to do somewhere. That's it, he told himself, concentrate. Feel the air passing in through the nasal passages. Banish all thoughts from the slate of the mind. *Damn! Why can't I be a news photographer instead of wasting time here?*

The first file belonged to a Mr. Sam Delgado.

Just before noon, Gatzo, who'd been sanctimoniously talking to the public on the phone most of the morning, came over and asked David out to lunch. They tried a new spot, an American-style cafeteria three blocks away, where the lines weren't very long. In a red-upholstered booth, Gene asked him about the demonstration.

"Well . . . I shot some good stuff. The cops got a bit wild. Oh, and I met this woman photographer."

Gene seemed excited for him.

"We just met, you know, nothing more. She's really something. Has a son who I haven't met. By the way, did you see the demonstration on TV?"

"Yeah, the protesters really provoked things. The news said they wouldn't let anyone in the building for Christ's sake."

David bit his tongue, not wanting to get into politics with Gene, so he went on to describe the demonstration. At one point he made a gesture that he immediately rescinded, a gesture that was at once feminine and seductive. He checked Gene but the clerk hadn't raised an eyebrow. David remembered times when he'd caught himself acting similarly with The Jock in the office.

Gatzo, his voice stumbling and head moving as if the cutting edge of his words, began talking about women. At an EST party over the weekend he'd met a woman in an early stage of multiple sclerosis where she was shaky. Somehow he'd managed to get rejected again, asking her to sleep with him fifteen minutes into their conversation. David pictured Gene as Goofy the Disney character, asking.

"What's wrong with that?" Gene was demanding. "God, I was horny. I was trying to be v-v-very u-up-front with her."

"You must be getting very frustrated, Mr. Gatzo." David wondered if he really wanted to get involved with a loser. But something was drawing him in — the older brother complex?

"Yeah, I get so h-horny sometimes I think I could screw anything on two or four legs."

"Pardon my directness, but have you thought of finding a hooker?"

"Not really. I got burned once while I was in the Air Force. I was all ready to come and I said something and s-s-stuttered and the stupid whore laughed. N-Needless to say, I lost it." Gene shook his head and looked off to the side.

"Next time don't talk — they say non-verbal experiences are richer."

David looked at Gatzo as they ate, trying to see him as a woman would. Was there anything at all about him that women might like? There had to be a few out there who'd take on a difficult guy as a mission in life. On the other hand David wondered why he was assuming that Gatzo was hetero. It could be that Gatzo was attracted to him.

On the way back to work a rather androgynous human passed them on the sidewalk. "Female," said David.

"Yeah, I guess so," said Gatzo, still dwelling on his disappointments.

"The shoes, the hair and the Adam's apple," said David. "If you see a woman with a big Adam's apple her name is Adam and not Eve."

"I've seen a few downtown," offered Gatzo. "Oh, I saw one in Merrill's Drugs a week ago. At least I'm pretty sure it was one."

"A drag queen? How could you tell?"

"I don't know. There was just t-too much funny about her. Her voice was too low and her face looked kind of coarse."

They strode past the lobby guard and rode the elevator up to work along with a real woman David wanted to undress. Back in his cubicle, there were even more files on his desk. He wished he could go home and masturbate, or at least lay his head on his desk and sleep awhile.

Something happened later that bothered him to no end. He entered the men's room at the same time as his boss. David quipped "The urge strikes again" as Vince allowed a grunt of agreement. David realized with a start that with only two usable urinals they would have to stand next to each other. They both unzipped, Vince with a strong, deliberate motion. After an appropriate interval David heard his boss pee against the porcelain. David pushed down against his bladder, waiting for at least a trickle. Sweating, he looked down to see only a small and wilting penis. Vince finished and zipped up.

"Guess I didn't have to go," said David. After Vince left, he peed generously and vowed to always pee in a stall in the future. His zipper seemed extremely conspicuous as he walked by Vince while returning to his desk.

After a stressful day at work, Natalie would come out of hiding again. Natalie could help him feel sexy and content. He could become sleek and exciting, even though there was no one around to appreciate him. Finally, Natalie could bring him to a pinnacle of pleasure. Then she all too quickly left. Sometimes when Natalie came out too much, even she couldn't stop the blues.

David knocked on the door of a house in the Haight Ashbury district. It was near dusk and an advanced coolness had settled down in the neighborhood of older stucco houses stacked together like books on a bookshelf. The houses all had upper and lower apartments above garages.

David knocked again and looked at the warm light filtering through the curtained window. Abruptly a child parted the curtain, looked at him intently, then went running, shouting "It's a man, mommy." Diane and a heavier and taller woman, introduced as Laura, shortly came to the door smiling.

"Hey!" he said, feeling debonair. The smells of good cooking reached his nose. He had come with an appetite.

As he entered, crayons, dolls and toys were everywhere. Only the kitchen seemed to be in order. He met Diane's son Bobby and Laura's two toddlers.

They all ate well around a circular table before putting the children to bed. Then the three talked and smoked some pot. David nearly forgot to show Diane the latest copy of the *Times* with one photo of hers, two of his and predictably the staff photographer's photo on the cover. Diane wanted to know all he could tell her about the *Times*, about Don the editor and office politics. David apologized for not being an insider.

He followed Diane and Laura into their living room to hear some new records. Wine and pot took their toll on him as he kept trying to be attentive. "Oh Jesus," he finally said. "The shape I'm in, I'm going to totally conk out any minute. What time is it? Can I use your phone to call a cab?"

"You don't mind if he sleeps here tonight, do you?" Diane asked Laura, the quieter of the two.

"No problem." Her hair was shorter than Diane's and fluffy, and she was more inclined to wear dresses.

He lay on the foreign-smelling sofa in the dark, under a comforter, listening to city sounds. After the pot, sleep came easily.

Later, he remembered reaching up with his hand to scratch

his nose. He'd been dreaming about walking through woods and a leaf had just brushed his face. He woke and for a wild instant couldn't remember where he was. Finally he recognized the front windows and the silhouettes of plants. He looked around. Then he spied Diane trying to hide below the side of the sofa, wearing a shimmering nightgown and wielding a long peacock feather.

"So that was you!" he whispered, trying to grab her.

"Hey now," she said, pushing him away. "I just came in to see if you were, well, sleeping."

"Well, I was, you know." He wondered why he was keeping up this tack of conversation.

"I thought if you were awake, we might, ah . . ." Diane let some of her long hair sweep across his face. "But if you'd rather go back to sleep—"

David regained his senses. "I thought you were just interested in newspapers and cameras." Diane put her hand over his mouth and slid onto the old, uneven sofa with him.

The sensation of having her, David wrote later, was like entering a tropical flower.

7

After the largess given him by Diane, David was more confident when he attended his third meeting of Maria Osaki's TA group. And just in time, as he had agreed to be one of those on the hot seat for this session.

Maria was late and her clothing atrocious as usual, but David was getting used to her. He worried about how he'd behave in front of everyone. Maybe he'd break down and cry. They probably wouldn't be satisfied until he'd belched up some heaving emotion. Most of all, would he finally have to say in public that he had a continuing love affair with women's underwear?

When it was his turn, Maria asked David why he was in the group. Why did she have to be so direct? He wasn't prepared to go so simply to the core. He preferred the indirect route, the mystery, the drama.

"I guess I'd say that . . ." he ventured hesitatingly.

"Yes, go on. You don't have to be shy here."

"It's my dad and I. We don't get along. We have a mutual

hate society. We're not communicating. My mother tags along with him. I should say that they're back in Ohio."

"How do you hate each other at such a distance?" asked Maria, pointing her ballpoint pen at him. "By telephone? Does he come out here much, or what?"

"Right now it's by letter," said David in a little voice.

"Sounds like you put some distance between the two of you. Just what do you fight about?"

"Could I break the flow a moment?" asked David. "I brought these photo albums with me. Since I'm a photographer I'm really into pictures — and I thought that people here could get a better idea of where I'm coming from if they saw them. Pictures don't lie."

"I'm not so sure about that," said Maria. "Most pictures are posed. Besides, what we're interested in most is what's happening in the here and now — what you're feeling now — not what happened twenty years ago when you were being potty trained."

There were a few titters. David had to smile. But there he stood with albums in hand, embarrassed, silently asking. Maria, grumbling, finally assented and while the albums circulated, argued with an attendee about not paying on time.

There were murmurs and pointing fingers as the albums changed hands. At one point, Rae, a woman whose obvious beauty had begun to fade, came in with her boyfriend, both slightly tipsy from wine. Maria calmly said she could stay if she toned down and her partner waited in his car. Rae went to look at the photos while Maria asked for comments. No one seemed eager to speak. David at once suspected that his life was so featureless that no one had an iota of interest in it. If only they knew. Or was the verdict so bad that they didn't want to hurt him?

Then Rae spoke up with the brazenness of a woman who knows she's speaking for the masses. "You want to know what's here?"

Maria began a motion to silence her but before she did, David said "Yes . . . please."

"Why, this is Anytown, America," pronounced Rae. The others in the circle nodded their heads, relieved that there wasn't an esoteric explanation. "This is like the family next door when I grew up. A typical all-American family in the forties and fifties. High school graduation, birthday parties, dad in his Army uniform holding a baby—"

"How does my dad look like to you?" asked David in a quivering voice.

Rae squinted pointedly at several pictures. "A strong man. Seems kind of like a he-man the way he sticks his chest out. He seems very proud to be in a picture with his baby."

David was flabbergasted. This he-man was the guy who'd generated such hates that David thought he could write a book of atrocities.

"Hmmm," he responded. "That's not the way I see him at all. I thought he was a real bastard a lot of the time. He could be mean."

Maria was becoming interested. She shifted to one side and looked up from the notes she'd been taking. "Like how was he mean to you?"

David put a bullet in his gun, picking his grimiest cartridge. He described the time his father had taken his brother and himself down in their basement and ordered them to rub mud all over their naked bodies because they'd kept playing in mud puddles. Maria told David to re-live the episode.

"I feel debased, as though—"

"Talk about everything as though it's happening to you now."

Talking to the group was like standing naked again. David worked to prevent his voice from disappearing altogether. "I . . . feel debased. My body is so white and skinny. My Dad is making us rub cold mud all over our naked skin in the cold basement, like in a dungeon. I can feel the cold floor under my feet. I feel like a Jew in a concentration camp being forced to do something that would take away my last ounce of self-respect. Why isn't my mother coming to stop this? She just peeked down the basement stairs at us and left without saying a word."

David noticed that no one in the group was shedding tears or running over to comfort him. And this was his worst story? Shouldn't this episode explain his being so fucked up?

"All right," said Maria, "here's what I see happening. The adult part of you, the part that makes plans, et cetera, is saying, 'I feel small and naked—my penis is small and naked.' The child part of you, the part that has feelings and emotions, says 'I hate my father.' And finally the parent part of you, which in TA means the instructions recorded in our head by your parents, is saying 'Rub mud on yourself'."

Maria continued — "Now I want you to act out your feelings against your father."

David was in an embarrassed daze — he had to come up with something. Recklessly he said "I'd tie my father to an overhead beam in the basement so he couldn't see me and I'd whip him. After that maybe he'd be tied to a cross and would rise up into the heavens or whatever."

"Anything more?"

"Yeah." David's mind was clearing. "Then I could be friends with my mother again." His eyes rimmed with tears he fought to hold back.

"Now try to act out the whipping of your father. Try to feel that you're actually doing these things to him."

Fearing that he'd become a spectacle, he said he couldn't go further. He sat wearily down while Maria complimented him on his progress. After a few seconds he found enough courage to look at the others. They — with the exception of a woman who smiled sympathetically — sat calmly as though this was their standard cup of tea. The next person stood up. David slowly let all the pent-up air out of his lungs.

Before he went to bed that evening he bloated himself with a huge hamburger and butterscotch ice cream. He was miserable the next day and nearly called in sick.

David became engrossed in what Maria Osaki could tell him about himself. In his personal transvestite alchemy of man and woman together, did his father play a part, this Zeus-like father who'd thrown lightning bolts down from the heavens? David developed enough interest to call Maria's office to try to set up private sessions with her. She was telling him new things and, as with his earlier fascination with Freud, his intellect was being prodded. Besides, as he wrote in his diary, he needed some attention from someone who cared a little.

When David entered the Sutter Street Medical Building on his first visit, the lobby resembled the foyer of a forties movie palace. Its slow elevator transported white-skinned old patients with vacant eyes. The plants in Maria Osaki's office were struggling, too, and her receptionist had bad teeth. As he waited, he looked out the window of the 39th floor and saw a grayish, smoggy city.

The meeting with Maria proved to be disappointingly short to David, who expected to spill his guts. Instead, she asked that he prepare a contract describing what he wanted to accomplish. Then she mentioned her fee. David nodded mildly, though he hadn't thought the bill would be so high. At the next meeting a week later, David unemotionally handed over a contract. When she finished reading, Maria looked at him with some surprise as a small smile played around his lips.

"What are you smiling about?" she asked.

"I smile this way sometimes when I get nervous."

"I read here . . . Suddenly you tell me you're a transvestite?"

"Yeah."

"The contract you've given me covers too much territory. We need more specific things to work on. We should chose between your relationships with women and the transvestite thing." She looked up at David. The smile was still there.

He looked away quickly. "I suppose we should."

He was a little boy again, being obedient, agreeable and nice. "Well, what's most interesting to me is my transvestitism. It's made me feel like an outsider. So maybe that's the part we should work on."

"OK. You're a transvestite. That means you get pleasure out of dressing in women's clothes."

David nodded solemnly.

"Sexual pleasure?"

"Mm-hmmm."

"Are you gay?"

"Not really."

"If I seem way out in left field on this subject it's because I've never had a transvestite in my practice. Or at least one who said he was. How long has this been going on?"

She chose the same words—*going on*—that his parents might have. "Back to the beginning of puberty, even a little before."

"And in the contract you mention liking to be punished and tied up. What do you want to be punished for?"

David fit comfortably with the detached, clinical way they were talking. They may as well have been two engineers talking about electronic circuits. He took his time formulating his answer.

"For being bad, for having broken the rules. Maybe for dressing up as a woman—I'm not sure. Also, hmmmm. There's something in the back of my mind. I guess I like to feel helpless before a woman, to have a woman lord it over me. To feel under the total control of a woman, to have a woman hurt me." He wondered if Maria was appreciating his honesty. *She must have very few patients who are so self-perceptive.*

Maria drew the now-familiar three circles—the ones labeled child, adult and parent—on her blackboard. "Let's look at this from the TA point of view, OK? I get the impression that it's the child in you that enjoys dressing. Your child is saying, 'I feel good when I dress'."

David looked on with a touch of skepticism while he fantasized having sex with her.

"Now your parent here," said Maria as she pointed to a circle, "is saying, 'Bad, bad. Boys don't dress like girls.' Did your actual parents ever say that to you?"

"Just once, the only time they discovered me dressed. They didn't say 'bad,' though. It's just the way they handled it. My father talked to me in the basement. After that I did everything secretly."

Maria looked satisfied. "That gives me the clue I need about your adult. Your adult says, 'I can enjoy this if I keep my parents from knowing. I'll just protect myself from my parents' prying eyes and disapproval.' So what we have here is quite a conflict between your adult and your parent." She drew arrows between the adult and parent circles. "Your adult protects your child from your parent."

Maria continued with more circles and arrows. What had begun as three circles rapidly became complicated by smaller additional adult and parent circles and many more connecting lines and arrows. Maria's explanations became more involved and confusing. David made a mighty effort to understand but the air in her office was stuffy and he had been farting. To make her think he was smart, he said he understood.

Soon the half hour was over—too quickly, when he considered the money he'd agreed to pay. As he waited for the elevator he again remembered vividly his father and the mud incident. There was a whole string of things his father had done. The trouble was that it was getting harder to hate him in his advancing years. David remembered his father's stories about *his* father, who'd treated him unfairly. Where would the chain of ill feelings end? Was hate burned into David too, to be passed on to a son of his own? David snorted when he thought of the possibility of getting married and having children—about as possible as strawberries on the moon.

Stepping out of the elevator into the strong light of day, David became immersed in street life—women with their provocative hair and dresses, men with their business suits and darting looks, fat and thin people, and always the rush of traffic. Somehow Maria's explanations, which had seemed so reasonable on the 39th floor, began to fade. Everything was so alive and vivid outside. He passed the window of a lingerie shop and stopped. Images of red lace and slender straps flooded his cerebrum, forcing all the data that Maria had given him to crash with a resounding thud. As a warmness passed through his veins, he went home and gloriously masturbated, then was depressed. In that state he called Diane.

8

Laura answered the phone. Her roommate wasn't in. That evening he finally reached Diane and suggested they get together over the weekend. "Why not tonight?" she asked. "Why don't I come over right now?"

"How about tomorrow night?" he asked, afraid she'd want sex when he'd already jerked off.

"Can't."

"Saturday?"

"Listen, I think I'd really like to come over now, if that's OK with you." At that he gave in and quickly tried to clean up, putting away his lingerie and making the bed.

He'd been fantasizing about Diane as a svelte photographer-woman to worship from a distance, someone who'd treat him a little coldly and who wouldn't get too involved. He most wanted a woman with whom he could share the ecstasies and mysteries of photography, a woman who was more proficient, perhaps, than himself.

She arrived wearing light brown corduroy trousers into leather boots along with a knit sweater. Her hair was pulled back, just like the first day they met. David poured wine.

"Two weeks ago I didn't even know you," she said, squeezing his hand.

"I know." He made a half-smile. "To be honest, I really wanted you over here tonight." *Even if not for sex.* "Because I started my private sessions with Lady Maria today."

"Who's this?"

"Her full name is Doctor Maria Osaki, ALC, BBMD, CRS, TNT, LNR. Just kidding. A transactional analyst. Do you know about TA?"

Diane nodded, sitting cross-legged on the large floor cushions in David's bedroom, and mentioned the time she'd briefly seen a shrink when her marriage was on the rocks. Sipping her rather sweet wine, Diane narrowed her eyes. "Something wrong?"

"Not much. Some old stuff with my parents I wanted to sort out." David wished he could tell her about the rest.

"Like what?" asked Diane.

"Oh, typical baggage. Anger at my father. Actually though, what bothers me is going to the therapist and reliving it all. It's like hemorrhaging."

"If this makes you feel so bad why the hell are you doing it?"

"Yeah, I've asked myself that. Someone said you have to feel worse before you can feel better."

Diane snorted. "Don't believe it."

David liked watching emotions pass through Diane's face as though she was a little girl. She never hid her thoughts.

The wine was beginning to work. David had begun talking about a lens he wanted to buy. Diane said, "Keep talking but lay on your bellows — I mean belly." Both laughed.

"On the bed?"

"Yes." She sat next to him and began strongly working his back.

"Minolta stuff is just as good as Nikon stuff. It just costs less, that's all," he said. Eventually Diane lay on him and kissed his neck teasingly. He began to writhe a little. She excused herself to the bathroom.

When she returned, nearly naked, she found an apparently

undressed David smiling, lying under bedcovers. She crawled in and reached down to touch his penis and found a curious bulge under slippery underwear. Holding up the covers, she saw him wearing panties. She clicked her tongue as she looked at him with a naughty smile. "Mr. Nunley, do tell! My, my, those panties really make you hard."

"Well, I like wearing them."

"You wanted to surprise me."

David moaned as she touched him through the slick material.

"Now my curiosity is going at 120 miles an hour. Do you wear these a lot? I mean, who would figure—Nunley the intrepid photographer wearing panties?"

"Mmmm. Touch me some more down there. Panties make it so much better." Then David ran his hand over her own panties and bent over to touch his tongue to the front of them.

"I'll bet you like my panties more than me," she teased.

"It's kind of like frosting on the cake."

Afterwards they lay naked and sated, panties lying crumpled on the floor. They held hands absentmindedly as her head lay on his chest. He liked the feel of her long hair against his skin. Finally she spoke softly.

"Don't you know it's women who wear panties and men the jockey shorts? Don't you know that crossing over isn't permitted?"

"Yeah. That makes it more exciting."

"I expected to find a kinda regular guy—hair on the chest, horny in the usual ways. But I guess no one's like regular anymore." She sighed. "Would you rather be a woman?"

David propped himself up on one elbow. "It would be nice to choose which body I'd be in each day. I'd just like to be whoever I want to be at the moment. That would be great."

"You make it sound so reasonable."

It was his turn to sigh. "There are fantasies, then there's reality. Unfortunately, I've got big feet and a not-very beautiful face."

"Aww, David, you're very good-looking. Don't put yourself down. But are you saying that you dress up completely as a woman? Have you tried to pass as a woman?"

David watched as his penis began to spring into life again. Diane noticed, then a look of discovery swept her face. "Those negatives you didn't want me to see—it all fits now—that was really you in those pictures!"

David blushed slightly. "Yes, dahling. Me as Natalie. I have a female incarnation I call Natalie."

"I have to compete with Natalie? Ohmygod. What other parts of your personality haven't I seen yet? You're a real puzzle to me."

"Oh, well. I've spent a lot of time trying to understand me. Sometimes I just stand back and say, 'How come I was dealt this deck of cards'."

"I feel like you've really trusted me by telling me all of this. It must take guts to tell someone."

"It's getting easier. When I was in high school I thought if anyone knew I'd die. I don't mean *die*, like girls say it. I mean I'd run away because I wouldn't be able to face anyone."

A week later, he delivered himself to Maria's office again. She wasted no time launching into her analysis.

"The part of you dressing up as a woman is the child in you. It's kind of like kids dressing up in their parents' clothes and magically becoming them for awhile."

David listened. The more involved they got with abstract circles and arrows on the ever-present drawing board, the more he lost track. He'd stopped asking her to explain things he didn't understand. Obviously, like a football coach at a chalk talk, she had everything figured out.

"The adult in you puts up with it but vaguely condemns it. Your parent, though, is where the conflict arises. Once you started taking your dressing seriously, your inner parent came down on the child in you." Maria went on with her circles to show how David's inner child related with his mother's inner child and his father's inner adult.

David was remembering that Gene Gatzo had said Maria was having marital difficulties and was living separately from Mr. Osaki, a businessman. David wondered how she would represent herself on the board.

Sterile. This diagram stuff is totally sterile. What I need to know is whether my dressing is OK or if it's bad for me. He didn't want to deal with transvestitism on the same level as being afraid of elevators or being shy. It had to be on the level of murder and mayhem — otherwise why had he tried to hide it so much over the years?

When his time was up he said, "Maria, I think I need some time to absorb the things you've told me. Some of it seems a little beyond me now. Also, I've been feeling more and more down after each session. It's been kind of hard on me."

Maria raised her eyebrows. "It's your decision, but I'll bet you're trying to escape your confrontation. You should realize that feeling bad shows you're coming to terms with yourself — that you're not glossing over it by masturbating all the time and feeling guilty."

But his mind was made up and after three private sessions he took himself off the hook with options of renewing later.

Diane came over on Saturday. They had nothing in particular planned. Laura had taken the kids to Golden Gate Park.

David ran his hands up under her sweater and felt her breasts under a skimpy bra. He was always a little surprised by the softness. The seductive bra ads he'd seen as a teenager made breasts look rather firm and pointed, and the water balloon breasts he used were resilient. He pulled up her sweater and looked — the bra was shimmery and stretchy. Diane reached down to touch his erection, saying, "You love it, don't you? You'd like to be wearing it."

"I thought about it. Too small."

"Are you wearing panties?"

He wasn't, and laughed with embarrassment. "How'd you like to go shopping for some sexy things?"

"Like what?" She smiled, looking conspiratorial.

David reddened. "Get some panties, maybe. Whatever."

"What a perve."

When they returned with shopping bags from Macy's she asked David to put on his new panties first. Shaking slightly, he completely undressed and pulled the drapes shut before solemnly slipping into the semi-transparent black lace. He had such an erection that it stuck incongruously out the side.

"It's not right unless I get my dick inside," he said half humorously. Finally he contained his bulge. Diane quickly undressed, went to his side with her lean body and began to caress his penis. Her fingers touched wetness through the panties.

"God, I can't stand it," he said, thinking he might be in heaven. At the same time he felt disappointed. When he was by himself his fantasies were pure. He could scan his imagination for whatever woman, whatever garment, whatever situation he wanted. Now he was with a flesh-and-blood woman with her own desires and her own imperfections.

He also halfway expected her to disapprove of all this—she ought to chastise and punish him. She put on her new pair of white panties, then provocatively rubbed his wet bulge against her less prominent one and touched her breasts to his chest. They both moaned.

David gathered up his courage and asked in a whisper close to her ear if she'd tie him up and whip him. It had been in the back of his mind all day but he'd delayed broaching it. His lust had taken over, though, and here she was, seemingly coming into his fold, apparently wanting to experience his sexuality. He held her tightly for a long time then stood back and looked into her eyes.

Diane returned the look. "You're kidding. No, you're not kidding. Look . . ."

This was the first time David had seen her embarrassed and at a loss for words.

"David, it's one thing to play house and dress up and all that, and fuck like rabbits. Ha! But dungeon stuff—"

David flopped down on his bed and lay there. "But you like pain a little bit. You like me to bite your tits. Haven't you ever played with a whip or anything before?"

"And you're telling me you have?"

"Just with myself."

"You're kidding. You flog yourself?"

"Now, come on. If you don't want to do it, just say so. I thought it might be fun."

"Do you ever wonder what *my* fantasies are? I mean, do I have a life?"

"Sorry. I know I'm always hung up on what I want. Tell me."

"My fantasies are so different from this material stuff you're into. Sometime I'll tell you — I'm not in the mood now. So I get to whip you. What will that do?"

"Arouse me, I suppose."

"I'll do it for you, with maybe just an teensie-weensie interest on my part. I mean, it seems like herding cattle with a bullwhip or something."

She began to lightly whack him across his white buttocks as he stood, hands tied to his closet clothes bar. He felt his erection becoming straighter and higher, now free of his panties, as though his penis was growing into a tree trunk.

"Surprise. I'm enjoying this a little," she said as she began to whip harder.

He began twisting against the ropes and finally asked her to stop. As she continued without letup he whined about getting hurt, then gave up all resistance and let her have her way.

"I never thought I'd enjoy hurting anyone like that. But it was kind of, well . . . interesting to make you beg. You're usually so unemotional . . ."

When he managed to disentangle himself from her amateur ties and came into the bedroom sheepish and with a still-stinging ass, she had him tie her down. In a mental fog that all of this was vaguely wrong, he tied cord around her thin wrists and spread-eagled her on the bed. He blindfolded her, then put on a bustier along with garter belt, nylons and perfume and told her to imagine he was a woman. As he approached her he noticed that his penis had been erect so long it seemed to be getting soft.

Slowly he straddled her and brought his genitals near her face. Then he drew the head of his penis along her lips. He ordered her to take it in her mouth, and after the expected refusals she lapped it up and engulfed it. Eventually he could wait no longer and entered between her legs.

Perhaps it was because he'd masturbated earlier in the day, he wasn't sure, but he didn't seem close to coming. Diane flexed her body along with his thrusts, a smile forming on her face. *She's not supposed to be enjoying this!* David tried to fantasize her whipping him again. She could be wearing a corset with sharp-pointed bra cups that cut into his chest. She'd coil a long wicked whip around his penis. He became harder for a few seconds before getting soft again. In desperation he switched fantasies and tried to imagine her forcing him to dress as a woman.

"Shit," he complained as he withdrew. Diane lay without moving, still blindfolded. "Goddamn, if we'd done it at the very first it wouldn't've been a problem. I went on too long."

"Poor boy," cooed Diane.

"I'm going to have to beat off," said David with tears in his eyes. He lay alongside her, embarrassed, and got himself hard. He went into her once more, angry, and got soft again. Diane had stopped moving. Finally he lay down with his head in the crook of her arm and masturbated until he came. He began to touch her clitoris with his finger.

"I think I'll go home," she said blankly.

He hadn't expected her to so completely confirm his expectations. He looked at her lying there, resolute and sure of herself. All animation had left her face.

"Don't you want to come?"

"Not any more. I'm weirded out."

"I'm going to leave you tied up. You know what they say about strange men you meet. Never trust strange men."

"Goddamn it, David, untie me now." She nearly shouted, working the blindfold off and looking at him fiercely.

"I like you this way—it's quite a turn-on."

"I don't care how you like me. If you don't untie me I'll scream my bloody head off and you'll never see me again. Now untie me."

David untied her before the neighbors heard. In a huff she dressed quickly and left. He looked down from his window as she drove away.

The next day David was riding the bus to work. He had a psychic hangover—exhilaration and depression were having their way with him. Some of his deepest fantasies—that had only been masturbation fantasies prior to Corky and Diane—were becoming realities. The combination of fantasy and reality was a disconcerting mix. He realized that he was uninterested in looking at women on the bus. Had he lost Diane and the relationship that had started so innocently? If only he hadn't soiled her.

David was reading a story in the *Chronicle* about a middle-aged man who kidnapped an eight-year-old schoolgirl, kept her chained in his house like a dog and did God-knows-what before being discovered. Then David chanced to read a notice posted in the bus—"PLAINCLOTHES POLICE RIDE THIS BUS FOR YOUR PROTECTION"—and began to imagine a pair of plain-clothes cops trying to arrest and remove him from the bus. At least they would *say* they were cops. He would insist not only on seeing their badges, but their photo IDs as well. They could charge him with resisting arrest if he acted too uppity, though. David pictured himself being forced into handcuffs and pulled off the bus, KGB-style.

"I don't think these are cops!" he would yell to the other passengers. "Is anyone going to help me? You, sir, are you just going to sit there? Why can't you get off your ass and help me?" He figured that maybe if he said just the right thing, eloquently and with heart, someone would jump to his aid. He practiced the various ways he might plead his cause. Then he wondered— would he come to the aid of anyone else in a similar situation? Or would he just take pictures?

9

Clearing his head of the bus fantasy, David arrived at work late again. Vince Grasso made a notation on his desk calendar. Later, David and Gene went to lunch at their favorite alley lunch stop, Lana's. The restaurant was underground and crowded, and the smell of fried food permeated the air.

Gene explained that he'd been on the hot seat in his TA group. Evidently he'd had a rough time of it—David had never seen Gene so emotional. "I t-t-thought those people liked me—"

David prepared to listen.

"They told me I couldn't r-relate to p-p-pee-people. J-Just when I thought I might get it on w-with this one woman there. I-I-I couldn't sleep a-at all last night. I feel about t-two inches high."

"Are you sure you're not exaggerating things? How could the leader let this go on?" David had never told Gene about his own sessions with Maria Osaki.

"All I know is it happened."

"Well, what the hell," said David, slouching down, "you

don't have to go back if it's so bad for you. You know, I'll bet they were saving up things to hit you with because they thought you were an easy target."

"What do you mean by that?"

"I mean that you stutter, that you're basically shy and don't mix too easily." David had been meaning to call a spade a spade for a long time.

Gatzo's forehead popped out big beads of sweat. "Look," he said angrily, "I can't do anything about my s-stutter."

David leaned over and asked him to speak softly. Several of the nearby diners were looking their way.

"And I don't have any problem mixing," Gene had to add.

"Ah, but it strikes me that you do it kind of forcefully — that maybe you really don't enjoy meeting people that much."

"I try, don't I?" Gene shook his head mournfully and sounded ready to cry. "Goddamn it, I try."

David resented Gene dumping his problems on him so emotionally. *We don't even know each other that well.* On the other hand, David considered that maybe he was just joining those who were kicking Gene when he was down. He, David, didn't need to be so honest.

"Maybe your EST and TA weren't the complete answers," said David.

Gene went on eating stoically, with body held erect. Finally he looked up. "I'll live."

David decided not to approach Diane for a while. After the bondage/SM debacle she had to think he was the world's worst freak-o.

Surprisingly, Gene had a Playboy Club card and he invited David along one evening. They both dressed up for the occasion and got a little drunk in the upper-Montgomery Street establishment, taking in the sexily-swathed bunnies who passed their table. David wished he could reach out and touch the tight costumes and run his hand down the bunnies' sleek nyloned legs — or better yet, become a bunny. He mentioned none of this to Gene, who was enjoying being serviced with drinks. Gene asked one of the bunnies if she'd been to modeling school. When Bunny Carol said no, he replied that it would help her walk more attractively if she had. He asked another if her mother knew she was doing this kind of work. Finally, he failed to tip.

An inebriated Gene exclaimed that by golly, the card had cost a lot but it was worth it. As they getting ready to leave, he asked David to come see his apartment sometime. Out of curiosity David said he would and before he went to bed that evening had a fantasy that he would visit Gene in drag and try to seduce him. He dutifully wrote about it in his diary.

Gene's apartment was a converted garage of sorts under a Sunset district home. After driving David there on a Friday after work, Gene led him into a nicely carpeted and appointed, if minuscule, studio apartment. They sat down after Gene showed him a manicured back yard accessible through sliding glass doors. He got a beer for David and began some small talk. David looked at a large poster of two gorillas hugging each other, with the inscription "If it feels good do it!"

It turned out that Gene wanted to talk about a girl he'd been dating, unbeknown to David. "Her name is Maryann. I knew her mother first — they live four houses away."

"How'd you get to know them?"

"Once I got a letter of theirs by mistake so I walked over to give it to them. After that, they went out of their way to get to know me — and they invited me over to dinner. An Italian family. You know I don't cook that well," said Gene, pointing to a kitchen sink full of dirty dishes, "so it didn't take much convincing. They have a daughter—"

"It's getting clearer," laughed David.

"T-There were t-two daughters in fact, and I never thought anything about them before I went over there. I'd just seen them driving their cars around and that was about it. So I went over one night for dinner and m-met this d-daughter Maryann who works downtown. She's four years younger than me."

"What does she look like?"

"Oh, kind of sexy. A little overweight."

"All that spaghetti. What then?"

"I took her out a couple times. We used her Mustang because she didn't like my car. You should've been there! She wanted to go to expensive restaurants. I think her mother thought

I was making real good money. Maybe I exaggerated my job — "

"Did you get anywhere with her?" David wondered if he was digging too deep.

"What it b-boiled down to was t-that she'd get lovey-dovey if I spent lots of money on her."

"So, did you make it with her?" David imagined Gene trying to win a prize at the test-your-strength booth at the county fair.

Gene rubbed his mustache. "No, no, no. S-S-Something happened. I went over for a snack at their place one night and the way they were l-looking at me was strange. I thought something weird was happening. I thought they'd . . ." — Gene paused, suddenly flustered — "I thought they'd poisoned the food, so I just left."

"You *what*? — they'd poisoned the food? How could you think that? Did they have a tarantula in the salad or what?"

"It was the way they were looking at me — half laughing, half like vultures. That's all I can say. There was no way I was going to eat what they had out. B-B-Besides, the food tasted funny."

"Jesus, did you accuse them?"

Gene finally broke out in a grin. "No, I wasn't sure enough. Well, anyway, we haven't talked to each other since."

On his way home, David knew what he liked about Gene. Gene was crazier than he was.

On his way to Diane's the following day, David felt so weak toward her that he debated on the bus whether he should turn back. He didn't like feeling dependent on her. Conversely, he thought he could leave her at any time. The tension was perversely enjoyable.

When he came to their house neither Diane nor Laura was there, but the kids were. Their mommies, they said, were shopping at the co-op grocery down the block. David tried to play children's games but decided he was twenty years too rational. Diane and Laura came in eventually, both looking nicely tanned and rosy-cheeked. Diane apologized, "David! I forgot you were coming!"

"We just talked on the phone this morning, you know." He remembered his crude attempts to apologize and patch up things, and remembered being surprised that she had seen her outburst as a temporary thing. She seemingly still wanted to see him.

Still, tears formed in the corners of his eyes. He knew how a dog felt when it put its tail between its legs and fawned before its master.

"You know how busy things get around here on weekends," said Diane, unpacking grocery bags. Also, she explained, their welfare checks had arrived.

That night after a cheery dinner where David tried to cover his sullenness, he and Diane went to her room. The walls had a fading tan complexion and large plastic milk boxes held her LP records. Thin wires connected a record player to cheap stereo speakers. There were three arty, immaculately-framed black and white photographs of her son on the wall. Her bed was topped only by a large spread-out sleeping bag over sheets. Diane's presence, though, made the room more than ordinary.

"I haven't worn this thing in years," she said, tossing him a black shortie nightgown from her closet. "It was a wedding gift from my poor husband. Why don't you try it on?"

David undressed and obliged, knowing how silly he'd look. He glanced at Diane in Levi's sitting on her bed, her knees pulled up against her chest in anticipation of the show.

He made believe that he was happy wearing the lingerie, which gave him half an erection. According to an unconsciously agreed-upon script he went over to admire himself in her mirror. He wanted to see a female self, but saw instead his hairy, slender body beneath the skimpy lace. When he turned to say something, Diane had coyly opened her shirt and was pushing up her bare breasts with her hands. "Do you like these, Davie?"

Davie again. Was he that transparent—was it that easy to see that wearing women's things made him into a child? He began breathing heavily. "Yeah, I would."

"Would you like to suck them?"

Yes, that would be exactly right. He made to come over, trying to imagine he was a woman. She motioned him to stop. She ran her hands down her sides and in a quick motion pushed down her Levi's and panties. "And what do you think of my bush?"

"I love it. It's so perfect."

He wanted her to order him to do something he couldn't quite define, so he stood there pleading with his eyes, just as he'd stood before Maria Osaki's group.

Diane had other ideas and left "for a toy." David heard some giggles elsewhere in the house before she returned with some oddball lengths of rope and string. Without a word, she tied him spread-eagled on her bed. Then she lit a candle, turned off the overhead light, and the room was completely quiet save for the low rush of a small gas heater. It was easy for David to imagine her as a sexy spider who had complete control over him.

Next she blindfolded him with a scarf and lay next to him. He could feel the warmth of her skin.

She tied a string around the end of his penis and played at pulling it to and fro, sometimes causing a little pain. The subtle feeling of it sometimes brushing his nightie was arousing and David began to involuntarily thrust with his midsection. At that, Diane stopped and touched his wet tip lightly with her finger. He was full of hot sex and yet tied up, unable to do anything.

Diane then left the room again and he lay there in the warm room in anticipation. And lay, and lay. Finally he thought he heard a few more giggles, distantly.

Then the door to the room opened, and there were the sounds of bare feet on a creaking floor. He tried to look out under his blindfold but couldn't. Soon the bed jostled and he felt one, then two, bodies lying next to his. After a barely-restrained giggle, Diane said, "I thought that three women might be better than two."

"The more the merrier," David croaked hoarsely. One of the bodies was squashing his penis.

In a battered Yellow Cab on the way home in the wee hours, David mulled over what had ensued. Diane and Laura had confirmed his suspicions by making love over and around him. He had tried to act blasé about it all. Their sex had seemed rather vanilla and he never heard or detected anything like a female climax. Every once in awhile someone would snuggle up against him or stroke his member a little. He had ached, hoping that someone would bring him to climax. Finally, when they released him, he went into the bathroom and came.

He remembered how the naked and pudgy Laura had cast a sly, smug smile his way when Diane removed his blindfold. What was that all about? *Diane's just toying with me.*

Before he went to sleep at home David had a fantasy that Laura had connived with Diane to recruit a man who could be rendered helpless. That brought back memories of teenage fantasies he'd had of women capturing him, tying him up, carrying him off and making him into a woman with a penis. Then he would live in an all-female society with the delightful mission of impregnating them surreptitiously.

With Gene Gatzo, there was always something new. Now, at work, he was explaining the Joel books. "They were written by this woman who has psychic communication with a spirit person named Joel. He told her about her past lives and all that." Obviously Gene's mood was improving.

David asked Gene if he'd given up with Maria Osaki. Gene said he was still going to the group meetings but his enthusiasm was with the Joel thing. He'd consumed the entire series of books, learning that Joel was a high-order being with esoteric knowledge of Atlantis, human history, fate, and just about everything else. David asked Gene if he thought he'd had a past life.

"I wouldn't be surprised. It might explain a lot of the way I am."

David loved to watch Gene when he got off on something. He would look excitedly off to one side when he talked and his eyes seemed to bug out of his head. As usual, he'd take his heavy glasses off and wipe them.

"Where are you going with this thing?"

"I'm not exactly sure but I really think there's s-something to it. I can see that you don't buy it."

David was surprised that Gene had noticed anything in him. "If there was a way to prove it I'd have no trouble with it."

"Well, haven't you read where people have been pronounced dead and then later were found to be alive? They said they'd been to a-another p-p-place like a h-heaven."

"I've never seen a place I'd call heaven. But, yeah, I've read those stories. I look at *National Inquirer* once in awhile."

Gene didn't laugh. "Well, the woman who communicates with Joel has been able to tell people things about their ancestors which she couldn't've known unless she had contact with another world."

Here we go again, thought David, here we go again. "Loan me one of your books, will you? I'm kind of interested, you know, in a scientific way." Gene took an exceptionally plain green paperback out of his briefcase, titled *Meetings With Joel, Part II*, by Grace Huebner.

"Maybe you were poisoned by someone in a past life," said David.

At first, Gene didn't understand. "Oh yeah. I didn't think of that." He pondered the possibility with a small smile.

"Or have you thought of the chance that you were a woman at one time?"

"I could've been, I suppose. Grace Huebner says she was a man in one past life in Italy and that she was in love with Joel who was incarnated as a woman."

"That's thick," said David. He looked up to notice Vince Grasso headed their way. "I suppose we're using up too much government time."

That evening David lay on his bed, alone, dressed as a woman except for wig and makeup. He began reading the Joel book. Coincidentally that evening he'd found lying on one of his tables a flier advertising a past lives session by a certain Ellen Havlik. He suspected that fate was making things happen for him again.

Right away, David felt better about this spiritual-mystical way of looking at life than the transactional analysis approach. This new outlook was friendlier—more about dreams and unseen things. Less industrial. Maybe there were past lives. After all, who was he to know? David moved his belly on the bed as he read and felt the artificial breasts inside his brassiere contact his skin. With his eyes closed he imagined that they were real breasts and toyed with the idea that he had been a woman in a past life— and that that person still wanted to be a woman inside him. He wondered if Joel had anything to say about transvestites or having been another sex in a past life. After much searching, he found a passage where the ethereal Joel was speaking through Grace. Joel had just finished talking about lines of energy that concentrated at certain points on the Earth's surface, including California.

Friend, this is hard to explain in terms of your concepts, but realize that people have both sexes in one body. Usually the dominant spirit matches the given sex of the body. However, from time to time if the spirit of a past life is particularly strong and of the opposite sex, and if the present person is vulnerable, that strong spirit may come to the fore.

The concept seemed reasonable enough to David.

Gene didn't need much persuading to join David in signing up for one of Ellen Havlik's sessions in Mill Valley. They drove over together on a Thursday after work and found Havlik's address on a quiet, shady street clogged with too many cars.

Twenty-seven people of all ages, sizes and persuasions had already congregated when Gene and David arrived. Most of them, David discovered, were there because they had read past lives articles in newspapers. Several told him that Ellen didn't waste time—she'd try to put the entire group under hypnosis that evening. The idea of being hypnotized for the first time made him nervous.

Ellen Havlik was a slender, cerebral woman whose face was marred by acne. Explaining that she was doing research for her Ph.D. by running the sessions, she exuded enthusiasm to a receptive audience. When she asked them to lay down en masse on her thick wall-to-wall carpeting, Gene looked like he was ready to meet God.

Ellen began to intone in a weird, high-pitched, occult-sounding voice, relaxing the bodies that a hectic civilization had sent her. After leading everyone into a feeling of weightlessness, she started counting back through the years to childhood, back through birth experiences and then into previous lives. David indeed perceived that he was going back in time in a poetic, dreamy state. He allowed himself confidence in Ellen.

At the end of the session, after they'd returned to their limp bodies, an amazing number of ex-Romans revealed themselves. One plump lady with a Slavic accent was sure that she'd been with Christ. A young man had been on the crew of a sailing vessel in the 1800s while another had been in Louis XIV France as a woman.

David himself had been an Indian in one of his lives. More interestingly, an Indian woman. He'd even seen the very bead design on his moccasins and the layout of the village where he'd lived.

On the way home David listened to Gene tell how he'd been a stone-age man. "Now that I think of it," said David, "the shape of your skull is like a Neanderthal Man's. OK, just kidding."

David tried to sound nonchalant when he mentioned about having been an Indian woman. In actuality, the possibility of having been a real down-to-earth woman wasn't as exciting as he'd thought it might be.

As he'd done with Maria Osaki, he decided to speak to Ellen Havlik about a private session, since he'd decided to follow up on this female personage. When he called Ellen the next day she discouraged him. There were so many articles to write and talk shows to go to, she complained, besides having to sift through data for her degree studies.

Finally, after he indicated more than a dilettantish interest, she gave him an appointment for a month later.

His next phone call was to Maria Osaki's office to cancel their relationship completely.

10

The following Saturday David was in the offices of *The Real Times* with a camera slung over his shoulder. Don Hill and the crew were still there, but David quickly learned that the newspaper had been sold. "I'm hanging on a thread," Don confessed, though he seemed relieved that the suspense was over. David asked about the new owners. The slight editor chuckled in the conspiratorial way that underground newspaper people developed. "It's a consortium of investors incorporated in the Bahamas. Kind of shadowy. Our esteemed owner must've made enough money to keep him happy in his old age."

David remembered the legends of how the former owner had gone from selling photocopied *Real Times* on streetcorners to creating a full-blown weekly newspaper.

"Here, have some cheap wine," said Don. David had seen many half-finished plastic cups around the office and the paste-up crew looked hung over. The newspaper, already a pale version of what it had been at its zenith in the late sixties, would forever change.

David stayed on to commiserate with Don. He realized that the switch would alienate him, David, from the paper. The new editor would likely be a guy wearing phony beads and white shoes, carrying computer printouts. For the memory, he snapped a quick shot of Don at his roll-top desk. Then the two of them hugged briefly, both a little embarrassed. David gulped the last of his wine and made for the door, grabbing a copy of the latest *Times* on the way out. The cover displayed a photo taken by none other than Diane of a nude woman meditating on a beach. A lover of hers? David wondered if she would try to get herself on the new staff.

When he got off the bus and walked the two blocks home, he picked up the day's mail and found a letter from his parents. They hadn't written for several months. Inside his apartment, he dreaded opening it. At least it contained his mother's gentle handwriting—

> *Dear David,*
>
> *Your father doesn't know I'm writing this. He wouldn't like it. Still, I want to write so you don't think we've forgotten you.*
>
> *He is still angry about what you told us. I don't know if he'll get over it. He's always been uneasy about homosexuality, so that's where it stands. You're his son so it's hard for him to accept. Sometimes he says that you're not his son.*
>
> *I want to tell you that mostly he doesn't understand you. I don't either. But I'm not writing to tell you to change. I just want to tell you that I love you and always will. Please allow your father some time. You can write if you wish—I won't show the letter to your father if you don't want me to.*
>
> *Love, Mom*

The last few lines were squished together on the bottom of the page, as was her custom. David had always read his mother's letters, for it was usually she who wrote, with trepidation. They were invariably serious, full of the small misfortunes of her group of friends. When he read the letters it was as though he was sitting next to her at the family's old kitchen table. She usually understated things—the mention of a breeze might indicate a hurricane. The few times his father wrote, the language was spartan and terse, without the shadings of his mother. The old man's handwriting resembled bent wires while his mother's was soft and delicate.

This letter complicated things. Now he was expected to re-establish contact again, if only with his mother. She didn't want to lose him. He supposed that there was something about him having been a baby inside her. Even so, David didn't feel an affiliation. He didn't think he needed her or them. He had coolly thought that if they died he wouldn't attend their funeral. They had nothing in common except the thin thread of tradition. They were getting old. Maybe he'd get around to writing in a month or so. He'd show them he could dish it out as well as his old man could.

David enlarged one of the photos he'd taken at the Civic Center demonstration—a non-violent one—and took it to the office to mount on his cubicle wall. Vince Grasso noticed the new picture. He wondered what it meant. David Nunley, employee, was always trying to be different in an obvious, raw way. Vince wondered how a regular clerk could have such pretensions of being a photographer. If David was that good, why wasn't he earning his living at it? David was always trying to show off, always thought he was special. He'd go off to eat by himself or with the quirky Gene Gatzo. Finally there were David's offbeat clothes, some of which Vince heard were from second-hand stores.

Vince had never mentioned it to David but once, while looking for a lost file, he had found a little shopping bag in David's desk. It contained three pairs of panties, a bra and several bottles of makeup. The way he pictured it, the panties and bra might be for a girlfriend, but no guy would buy a woman makeup. Vince had only mentioned it to his wife. They had laughed about the possibility of the stubborn David being gay or a closet drag queen.

David certainly did get rebellious at times. Sometimes Vince could see the anger in his clerk's eyes. In the end, though, David usually went along with the program. His work was better than average—if only he didn't call in sick so much. Vince's eyes went back to David's photo. Below it David was working on file entries.

Diane and Laura welcomed David with knowing smiles as they let him in their old front door. It was a weekday evening and they were putting their children to bed.

"What've you got?" asked Diane. David was carrying a blue nylon athletic bag. "Some goodies," he replied with a furtive smile.

On the way over, and now in the apartment, he felt cold, to the point where he left his jacket on even in the house.

After some wine and pot, Laura and Diane escorted him back to Diane's bedroom. "It's Rocky Horror Show time," said Diane, opening his bag. "Look at this. You've outdone yourself, David." She pulled out a long, black, boned corset.

At the same time, David pulled down his trousers to show them the stretch-lace panties he was wearing, complete with half an erection.

David proceeded to dress up, wearing the corset and a dress of Diane's. They put a little makeup on him and he pulled on a long wig he'd brought. This was always what he'd wanted—so close to his fantasy of being captured by women and turned into one—but he was developing a major headache and queasy stomach.

The three of them lay on Diane's bed. Diane was reaching under his dress while Laura, like a basking cat, was watching. He pulled away.

"What's the matter?" asked Diane.

"I'm just not into it."

"Of course you're into it, buster," she kidded. "Don't act like a vestal virgin."

"I'm sorry. I just don't feel like it. I don't feel that well."

"It must be your time of the month, Natalie."

"Don't get all catty with me, Diane. I could be getting sick. Besides, I probably wouldn't even come, anyway, like last time. I'd just be frustrated while you two get off on each other."

"So that's it. Plain simple old jealousy," said Diane.

"I'm sorry. I'm not into it any more."

"I'm not into it any more," mimicked Diane. Laura reached over and touched his forehead. "I think he's got a temperature."

He dizzily put his accouterments in his bag and went to the bathroom to wipe off his makeup. Diane came in and looked concerned.

"I'm sorry I teased you, David. Maybe it won't work out with us—you and Laura and me. Besides, you always seem like you only half enjoy dressing. Like, you're guilty about it."

David mumbled an incomprehensible answer. He was sweating profusely.

Diane drove him home. Without Laura, she wasn't so bad. On the way she mentioned a transvestite group she had met at the *Real Times* office. She was thinking of doing a photo story about them.

He took aspirin, then allowed his body to sink into bed. As he floated and slowly rotated in space before falling asleep, he wondered if getting sick was a payback for being degenerate.

"David." Diane was calling, three days later. "How are you?"

"I'm in bed sick. Catching up on reading."

"Now we know why you were so out of sorts. Say, I've got to tell you about the transvestite meeting I went to, the one I covered for the *Times*."

"Oh yeah, you said you were doing that."

"You don't sound very interested."

"I suppose I should be. Well, what was it like?"

"Hmmm. I wonder if I should even tell you."

"Stop teasing."

"OK then. It was really something. This was in Millbrae. These guys are really into it. It was like a Tupperware party or something. You would've liked it. They were nice people—had a sense of humor. Some of them even looked sharp."

"Were there any real women there?"

"A few wives and girlfriends."

"Hmmm."

"I got in good with this one guy there, which wasn't easy because a lot of the transvestites were afraid of getting their photos or names in the paper." She went on to tell about a Korean-American electrical engineer who lived in San Francisco. "He said you should come to a meeting. He'd like to meet you."

11

Ellen Havlik, the past-lives person, welcomed David politely. She seemed more casual and self-assured than before, and her acne didn't bother him as much. There was even something erotic about her and David wondered if she had any possibilities.

Ellen apologized for being on a tight schedule and after glasses of wine they got down to business. David turned on his tape recorder, lay down on her soft sofa and relaxed as her ethereal voice took over.

Again she guided him back through his childhood, back beyond several previous lives. His eyes were closed and his replies to her questions were slow and languorous.

"You are now in a time ten years before your birth," droned Ellen as her voice seemed to merge with the passage of much time. "Where are you?"

David vaguely remembered that all of this was being tape recorded, so he wouldn't have to worry about retaining anything. "I see a lot of the color blue," he offered, "and I see much green, the green of trees."

"What else do you see?" Ellen's disembodied voice seemed to be coming from a faraway, dark place.

"I see people—they must be Indians. I'm in a village of sorts next to some trees—pine trees with tall, straight trunks."

"What are you wearing?"

"Leather. Soft, like doeskin."

"Are you a man or woman?"

"A woman." A sexual twinge passed through his body.

"Do you know your name?"

"Pem-on-quin, I think. Just Pem . . . on . . . quin."

Where am I getting this stuff from? He figured that either he was a good bullshitter or else this information was coming from . . . The Source. He went on and on, providing details, years, locations—in the Four Corners area of Arizona—and costumes. He provided a story first of happiness, then of privation as soldiers wearing deep blue uniforms forced her tribe to move. Pem-on-quin had a husband and told of making love. Ellen didn't show any emotion during the elicitation of these memories. When she finally brought David back to the present he discovered he had covered so much the recorder had run out of tape. He was proud of himself.

To his amazement, after some library research, David found that he had described a Navajo hogan hut perfectly. Also, he learned that the Navajo reservation occupied the Four Corners area of northeastern Arizona.

He told the story to Gene the next day at lunch, mentioning a plan to visit the Navajo reservation to "do a story for one of the magazines or the Sunday supplement. Maybe this would give me a break on starting in as a photojournalist."

"A woman, huh? So you really think you were a woman in a past life. That's something."

"Blows my mind to think I might've made love with a man at one time."

Gene made an effort at eating and was silent.

"So you're actually taking your vacation in Arizona, then?" asked Gene.

"The last two weeks in June."

"Well, I ask because I might need a place to stay. I'm going to have to move about then." Gene's face darkened. "D-Damn the landlord—he wants to move his niece in. I've been s-so g-g-good for the place. I've been quiet, kept it up, w-worked on the back yard. This is the thanks I get." His eyes moistened. "I mean, I might need a place ta-ta-ta-temporarily if I can't find a new apartment by then."

"Don't see why not," allowed David. Gene could watch over things, feed the fish and so on.

> *Dear Mother,*
>
> *Thanks for the letter. I'm not going to have a sex-change operation, if you've ever wondered. And I am not a homosexual.*
>
> *I don't know what to write. Yes, I'm still ferment-ing (working) at the VA. Still a lowly correspondence clerk.*
>
> *And yes, I still dress as a woman sometimes. I've been coming out of the closet with it, you might say. People are more accepting here in California. I don't know if you ever realized it or not but I was dressing on the sly at home after I was ten or so using your clothes.*
>
> *It's not something I do deliberately to shame you but it's something that is organically necessary for me. For the future, who knows? Believe it or not I actually would like to get married sometime.*
>
> *I'm taking a vacation in June to try to verify a past life of mine.*
>
> *Cheers,*
> *David*

As he dropped the letter in his mailbox, he found a newly-delivered letter inviting him to a party a week later.

The invitation's directions led David to an old second story space in the South of Market area which served as the office for a stock photo agency called Pacific Image. The hostess and manager of day-to-day affairs for the company was Sam Waggoner, an affable, muumuu-clad woman.

It was a party for the old staff of the *Real Times* who'd pretty much left the fold after its sale. Diane was there with her son, being kidded about working for the new owners. Rounding out the crowd were venerable bearded writers and cartoonists who still looked very hippie- and sixties-ish. Sam was making the rounds of the photographers trying to drum up more stock photos for her business.

David was rescued from his unease by a woman he'd met several years previously. Jeanette had the sloe-eyed face of a princess and was as entrancing as before. He learned that she worked for an upscale food catering place besides being a textile artist. They exchanged phone numbers.

Diane seemed friendly enough and talked to David briefly about everything but ropes and humiliation. Later David noticed her talking to a slight, wispy-haired photographer—probably another feast for the spider lady and her partner. David hoped she wasn't telling anyone about Natalie.

There was the lament at the party that the photographers were all getting older and going either more commercial or more into the woodwork. As he left, David thought that he should be on the side of the entrepreneurs. He should be out there capitalizing on his talents, too. At least, he told himself, he could follow up with Sam and her offer to broker some of his photographs.

Upon returning home that evening, David finally dared to call the transvestite whom Diane had met at the Diana Society meeting. That person gave David the mailing address of the society and suggested that they go to a meeting together.

David tentatively joined by mail, hoping to avoid another confession-oriented group experience. The first exposure to the society was through their newsletter, *Gender Expressions International*. Part of the publication devoted itself to stories written by transvestites—or TVs—and transsexuals about their experiences in the outside world. David now knew that his own story was not an isolated one.

He read the story of a man who lost favor with the other

members of his paramedic team when they found out he was a TV. Then his wife and children left him. After yet more troubles, the man finally found a woman who accepted him.

Then there was the story of Lisa, who'd lived as a woman for several years and finally had a sex-change operation in Colorado. She had assumed that once she was a woman she would be attracted to men and live with one—but no, she was still attracted to women so she called herself a post-op lesbian.

There were great hopes and disappointments in these stories. Gender and crossdressing came up more often than sex, though several stories were quite graphic. When he looked at photographs of the writers, David saw some disappointing types with bad makeup and big shoulders. The quasi-women attempted sexy poses. On the other hand, there were photos of truly gorgeous transvestites.

Finally he was ready to take the leap and called the transvestite he'd connected with earlier. They met in a bar-restaurant in David's neighborhood, then proceeded to the TV's apartment. Jimmy Kim was a somewhat rotund Korean who often laughed unexpectedly. After some small talk, Jimmy took out his photo album and showed pictures of himself in drag. David didn't say much, not being impressed, but he did arrange to go to a Diana Society gathering with him. Jimmy assured him that there was nothing to it—Jimmy would drive and they could dress at the party, or as some did, just come and remain dressed as men. David thought he might as well dive in and attend in drag, something he was ripe for.

All during the week before the party David thought he would die of heart failure. What would he wear? He changed his mind a dozen times. What would the others be like? Would they laugh at him?

Jimmy picked him up and they drove to Millbrae with their neatly-packed bags of clothes and makeup. In the excitement David began to enjoy him. "Damn," he said, "I never thought I'd be doing this. I'm so charged up I could pee my panties."

Jimmy snorted. "You get used to it after awhile."

The meeting house, in a quiet middle-class neighborhood at dusk, was surrounded by cars. David wondered how much the neighbors knew. He thought he must be part of a crime, but what an intriguing crime! Like attending a communist cell meeting in *I Led Three Lives.*

The Diana Society's hostess welcomed them at the door, a friendly woman with a man's etched face under makeup. She graciously introduced them to several of the fifteen or so transvestites and their friends inside. The TVs were sipping wine and seemed to be acting as women even if there were minor physical discrepancies, with one glaring exception. An older transvestite was speaking in a loud man's voice and laughing heartily, a Fellini caricature. David was taking a quick course in how and how not to act as a woman.

He and Janet, as Jimmy called himself, went to a long bathroom to dress. He saw Janet unhesitatingly slipping into pantyhose, his leg hair and penis squished underneath. David nervously put on tights, a padded girdle and his favorite bra. Breathing fast and with nervous stomach, he added a tight body shirt and finally wrapped a Thai sarong around his waist. When he finished his makeup and adjusted his long wig he looked in the mirror. *This is how Cinderella felt!* David was in a dream. There was perfume in the air, soft lights and the expectation that anything might happen.

He opened the bathroom door and tentatively walked out into the living room. *Well, the sky hasn't fallen down.* He expected all heads to turn but only several noticed him. One tall, heartylooking woman came over with a smile and spoke in a strong English accent.

"Hi! I saw you when you came in! You look so nice! I'm sorry, I don't know your name." She dressed conservatively and her hair was well-arranged.

"I'm Natalie. I came with Janet."

"I'm Darlene. This is your first time at the chapter, isn't it?"

"My first time ever in public," said David, trying to sound soft and feminine. He'd seen himself in the mirror as a woman and now his personality was slipping into the mold. He was becoming Natalie, a somewhat shy, demure creature who felt sexy and curvaceous. Looking down, he saw the double rise of breasts as they pushed healthily against his bodyshirt.

"Oh, I love it," said Darlene as she hugged Natalie and held her sweaty hand. She introduced her to the crowd and proposed a toast to "this gorgeous Natalie who's coming out for the first time tonight."

There was a warm glow in the room. Wine and smiles flowed easily. Natalie was glad she'd come. She took some photos of the TVs, including a group portrait. The highlight of the evening was a makeup demonstration by a real woman who sold cosmetics. She acted as if she was selling to another bunch of housewives.

Jimmy had changed back into male attire for the ride home but the wine had made Natalie more adventurous and she remained dressed. The Korean was nervous — "What if the police stop us?"

Just after midnight Natalie unlocked the front door to her building, crept lightly up the stairs and entered her apartment, hoping and not hoping that someone would see her. She began the time-consuming process of removing all traces of makeup. The silent and darkened apartment and the distant sounds of cars in the night were at odds with the tingling electricity in her body.

The second meeting of the Diana Society convened in San Jose at night. It was a combined meeting for all three chapters in Northern California and tended toward society business. David went with Jimmy. Among veteran attendees there was some infighting and disagreement under guise of Robert's Rules of Order. David-as-Natalie stuffed herself at the snack table while listening to old-timers who looked and sounded like bewigged male English barristers.

Natalie, wine in hand, eventually overcame her shyness to talk to a TV she'd been eyeing at the other end of the food table. This young and slim person dressed tastefully and looked convincingly female. Her face and movements indicated intelligence. She wore a shoulder-length wig that framed her face nicely, and a stylish blouse with a slim, dark skirt. Her breasts were understated.

"Hi, I'm Natalie. I think I'd like to meet you —"

"I guess I'd say the same." The TV smiled. "Well, I'm Karen from San Francisco."

Natalie liked her voice. A little maleness showed, but she could pass on the street. "I'm from the city as well," Natalie said, wondering why she adopted such stilted language. "I hate to say this, but the meeting's kind of boring."

"Yes, gawd, I'm glad someone said it," said Karen. "So far it's been an absolute desert here. I mean a *desert*. The only thing that's kept me here is the food and wine and the fact that my ride won't be by for an hour or so."

"Some old men in skirts."

"Politburo in drag."

Natalie reached out and slipped an arm lightly around Karen's waist. Karen mmm-ed but Natalie pretended not to hear. She complimented Karen's taste in clothing.

"You're not so bad yourself."

"I'm just a beginner—I'm learning. Pardon my curiosity, but who brought you?" asked Natalie.

"Oh yes. Who brought me. I have a girlfriend, Jean, who you might say is very supportive of my lifestyle."

"How long have you known her?" Natalie wanted to be more spontaneous.

"Oh, jeez, I think it's about a year now. Before her I was going with a woman for three years. I didn't tell her about my dressing at first, then when I did, ka-boom. She tried to accept it after the shock, but it really never worked. But Jean—I made sure she knew from the first. She's into the scene—helps me dress."

"Sounds like an angel."

"She stays with me most of the time—even shops for me. It's so nice to sleep with her with my nightie on."

At that, another woman interrupted. "Hi, I'm Roz from the Stockton chapter." She eyed both of them. "Well, I hate to butt in, but I need to ask if you like the name of the society as it is. Some of us from the Valley Chapter would like it to be Genesis. 'Diana Society' sounds too cutesy-cutesy to us."

There was something confusing about Roz. She had real, long hair, but it was oily and had dandruff. Her dress was out of style—too short, too tight, like something one might see at a back-country bar.

"Oh, I think it's fine," said Karen with a mischievous smile.

"Which one is fine?" asked Roz.

"I think it's all fine."

"I think we ought to call it the American Legion Auxiliary," teased Natalie, tossing her hair around with a flip of her head.

Roz could see she wasn't getting anywhere.

"By the way," said Natalie, "are you living as a woman all the time?"

"I'm a true hermaphrodite, mostly a woman, and I'm married to a guy." She threw up her hands in resignation, turned abruptly and walked away, leaving Karen and Natalie looking at each other blankly.

Natalie changed back to David at the meeting. After Jean picked them up, he ended up at Karen's apartment in the Union Street district of San Francisco. Jimmy Kim had been peeved that David was leaving with someone else.

Karen and Jean's apartment was a comfortable place with big, lush plants, primitive art from the South Pacific and two lovable parrots. Artistic lighting dramatized it all.

David sat in a comfortable breakfast nook with Karen and Jean. Jean, a nurse from the Philippines with a difficult-to-pronounce last name, seemed quiet and relaxed—a woman in her twenties with long black hair and tranquil eyes. Ever since he'd been a GI in southeast Asia, David had been an especially soft touch for Asian beauties.

The wine they sipped was from a prestigious vintner. Jean was talking in a low, melodious voice.

"Karen's a doctor, a pediatrician."

David had wanted to know. He'd wanted to ask Karen at the meeting but didn't, since asking about occupations seemed such a male hangup.

"We have to be careful about where Karen goes dressed because if the word got out—"

"Karen never goes to the office dressed," chuckled Karen, "though Karen would like to very much."

"I wish I'd seen you in drag," said Jean to David. Then, turning to Karen— "How does he look as Natalie?"

"Very, very nice."

David complained, "My makeup needs work. I've had to learn it all by trial and error." He described his times with Corky and Diane and how he'd connected with the Society. Then he asked the two how they'd met.

Jean explained that she'd come to Karen's office as a temp. He was the first doctor who'd ever attracted her. "You know, I'm bi,

I'm a switch-hitter."

"Sometimes she goes out to women's bars and picks up some-one," explained Karen, whose male name, Robert Vitriano, was only used professionally.

David couldn't resist telling about his upcoming vacation and his search for a past life as Pem-on-quin. Intrigued, they made him promise to report back. When he left in the wee hours, Karen hugged him and kissed him on the cheek, and Jean exchanged a more restrained hug. She seemed very soft and yielding. They had smoked some pot and David made his way home in the dark quite elevated and happy.

12

David packed his bags with camera paraphernalia, past-life notes and maps, not forgetting a pair of panties, and left his house key with Gene Gatzo before catching an AMTRAK train in Oakland.

As David reclined in his train seat, looking at flatlands and occasional cattle whiz by, he recalled hiding his women's things, negative files and diaries deep in his apartment closet. *If he finds the stuff, he's in for a shock.*

David had detected a certain dependence on him by Gene in recent weeks. Gene was still having no success with women. He'd go on one, maybe two, dates before getting the heave-ho. He'd tried ads in the local singles newspaper advertising himself as "a good-looking professional" and had received a few replies. Another thing was that Gene only wanted the best-looking women. When David advised him to lower his standards, Gene was offended. Ah, that impossible Gene. David wondered what kind of team the two of them made, what kind of Laurel and Hardy or

Dean Martin and Jerry Lewis.

Only a block from the train station in Gallup, New Mexico, David checked into the worn-down Arlington Hotel. He walked to his room and immediately masturbated. With too much on his mind the orgasm was unrewarding.

The next morning he boarded a passenger and mail bus and went via a meandering route into the hot and dusty Indian reservation. He'd read up on the once-warlike Navajo, a tribe that had settled down to become sheepherders and weavers.

After many stops at tiny post offices, David left the bus at Window Rock. He was frightened, sure that the search wouldn't pan out and that Pem-on-quin was a trick of his imagination. Yet, what if she wasn't? He walked aimlessly by the earth-colored buildings of the tribal-owned town before he saw a library. Inside, he finally worked up the nerve to ask a young Indian librarian if there was "a name like Pem-on-quin in the Navajo language."

She replied seriously that she didn't think so, but that he might go see "Roger, in the museum. He does research on the Navajo."

This is it, David told himself as he cautiously walked into the building, which resembled a conventional white man's museum. In fact, almost everything at Window Rock said "white man," especially the vast and well-stocked supermarket.

An attendant pointed David toward a rear room where Roger worked. Walking down a hall past mounted animals and Indian art, he entered a pine-paneled room with a long meeting table formally surrounded by padded chairs. David's body was trembling, he hoped imperceptibly, as he approached two Indians—a mid-sized, bulky young man and an older, leaner fellow. Roger turned out to be the former, a gentle, reserved person who spoke slowly, quite the opposite of the inebriated Indians David had seen in Gallup. David and Roger shook hands.

David was sure that he was going to ask the strangest question ever asked in Window Rock as he introduced himself and said he was from San Francisco, which he hoped would impress them. He tried to leapfrog his nervousness by launching directly into his mission.

"What I'm going to tell you probably sounds far-fetched, but — have you ever heard about past lives?"

The Indians shook their heads no. They weren't smiling, laughing, or showing any emotion beyond polite curiosity.

"It's the idea that people were someone else before they were born into this life. Like if I died now, I might be reborn later as another person."

Roger and the other man looked at him intently, not fully comprehending.

"Well, I was hypnotized and came up with the memory that I was an Indian woman living in this area in the 1800s, in a past life."

After some thought, Roger made a motion with his head to indicate he understood. David, relieved that he was taking this seriously, continued. "What I came for was to ask about her name, to see if it's a Navajo name. The closest I can come is . . . Pem-on-quin." He wrote it on a memo pad.

Roger furrowed his brow and looked at his taller friend. "It doesn't sound like Navajo."

David wondered if they were telling the truth. What would they think? Would they want the Navajo image tarnished by a brash white man who claimed he'd been a Navajo woman? The two Indians discussed the name. No, definitely not Navajo. Perhaps it was from the Pima language in southern Arizona — there were many different languages among different tribes.

Before he left, David showed them the drawings he'd made of pottery and beadwork designs he'd seen while under hypnosis. Roger kept saying, "Indian, but not us."

Back in Gallup, David felt lighter. He knew he wouldn't pursue the thing further. He'd dared himself and had done what he'd come to do. So he went out on the warm and dusty streets after dark and treated himself to a tasty dinner and an action movie. The next day he took a tour of the cliff ruins at Canyon De Chelly and came back tired to the still-hot hotel. The day after that was spent taking pictures of rusted car hulks, tattered sofas and eviscerated TV sets out in the desert.

Gradually a great emptiness filled him. He returned to lie on his bed in the heat of the afternoon and napped naked under a ceiling fan with the shades pulled, burying his face in a pillow. In a stupor of sorts, he went out for a meal and came back too depressed even to masturbate. He slept fitfully that evening, wallowing helplessly. In his light sleep he woke up after each of his dreams, thinking about each one.

In one, he was in a penitentiary cell full of gray, four-drawer files. One of the file drawers held his secret cache of lingerie and was kept closed, but some telltale bit of silken material always seemed to hang out.

Later in the dream energy was building among the prison inmates for a breakout. During a mass escape David went with the inmates so they wouldn't think he was against them, but once they breached the walls there was no place to go, just endlessly-flat, arid landscape. David stood and watched as the other men kept fanning out into the sparse, dry brush.

David woke at four a.m. and couldn't sleep. So he turned the lights on and took photos of the worn room with its old chairs, quaint pictures and rusty sink. Then he set his camera on self-timer and took nude pictures of himself in frowning poses using a wall mirror set up behind the tripod. He looked gaunt and stiff. Finally, photo-tranquilized, he was able to sleep another hour. When the day's new light began to creep in under the drawn window shade he had a desperate need to go out again photographing. This time he decided he'd head out in a new direction toward some low hills.

He walked down Gallup's main street with a canteen and wide-brimmed hat, feeling conspicuous next to auto traffic and early-rising Indians. The sun was high enough so that it warmed him. Transparent cotton puff clouds spread themselves uniformly over the sky.

He began walking along railroad tracks. A distant dirt road appealed to him, but a long, wide ditch of stagnant water fouled with oil and other refuse stopped his progress. Along its sides were tall stands of dry brush that seemed impenetrable. As David wondered how he would cross it, a cloud passing over the sun made him look up. The clouds had dramatically increased in size.

He had been standing still for a few minutes when a splat of water hit his back. After more splats, minor sprinkles gradually became a heavy downpour. David retreated under the eaves of a nearby corrugated-metal railroad shed. Sheets of rain beat into the dry ground with a vengeance. He looked around him next to the shed and saw old torn clothing, spread-out cardboard and empty cans and bottles. *I guess hobos still ride the rails.*

Just as he began to allow himself to enjoy the rain he detected the pervasive odor of shit. *Yes, definitely shit. They must take their shits here.* While idly thinking about hitching rides on freight trains, he brought a boot up so he could scratch his ankle. Attached to the sole was a clump of almost-fresh brown stuff. *I'm standing in shit. Dear God, the climax of my trip.* He began laughing and stomping his feet. *Mysticism. I'm standing in it!*

At that moment a switch engine went by on one of the many tracks. The engineer had been watching the presumed hobo with some amusement until David returned his stare. Then they both looked away.

David returned home on the next AMTRAK. He had discarded his toothbrush after using it to clean his boots.

The Bay Area was its old workaday self as he got off the train in Oakland and boarded a bus. While crossing the Bay Bridge he was uninspired by the hazy high-rises of San Francisco. Even the suspension portion of the bridge with its graceful cables failed to bring out the usual spark in him.

He'd had plenty of time to re-think the trip. Now it seemed a travesty. The poetic idea of Pem-on-quin had been replaced by the idea of Natalie as a whore. He only wanted to go home to rest.

As he climbed the carpeted stairs to his apartment he remembered with a start that he was returning early and that Gene might still be staying there. Maybe when he walked in Gene would be beating off! No, it was a weekday and Gene would be at work. Good old reliable Gene who never called in sick. David opened the apartment door, smelled the stuffy air, set his bags down in the foyer and went to the refrigerator to get a beer. In his discontent he wanted to stop thinking and watch TV.

Prominently taped to the side of the refrigerator was a sheet of yellow paper with a PLEASE READ printed in large felt tip pen letters at the top. David's heart skipped a beat. He knew instantly what the message was. Taking it like a letter from his parents, he sat on his bed with his back against the wall, swished some beer around his mouth, girded himself, and read —

> *David, I stayed here 3 days while you were away. Thanks for letting me stay.*
>
> *David, I found all of your women's clothes and put them in a duffel bag. I think that you should destroy them or give them to Goodwill. I don't know what you think you're doing, dressing like a woman like the perverts downtown.*
>
> *I looked up to you for a long time. I thought you were a great guy for a friend. I accidentally picked up a photo album from your bookcase that you probably didn't want me to see. At first I thought the pictures were of one of your girlfriends.*
>
> *Now I can see how some of your talk about queens, etc. was just playing with me. You must have thought I was pretty funny. I don't plan on talking to you again and I'd appreciate it if you'd stay away from me. I'm going to stay in a hotel until I find a new place.*
>
> *You're basically a nice guy and have no trouble attracting the girls. So why do you want to drag your name through the mud by being a pervert? This really makes me sick.*
>
> *Eugene*

David let out an exasperated sigh and a grin briefly appeared on his lips to accompany the tear that burned its way down his cheek. He had to admit he was blown away. He always knew that someone would hit him in the soft underbelly of his guilt. Of course he'd set it up. He knew that Gene looked up to him and would try to find out more about him — like guests who peek into their hosts' medicine cabinet.

Well, now Gene knew. Cheese is too rich for mice but many have sampled it in a mousetrap. David chuckled derisively. Obviously, Gene needed to learn more about the ways of the world.

Still, Gene wasn't a very resilient guy. Maybe he, David, was Gene's only real friend. He hoped that Gene would bounce back. He knew that working in the same office with him would be tense for awhile, especially if Gene told anyone.

Had touching the lingerie aroused Gene? Conversely, David checked to see if his buddy had gone berserk and thrown away anything. He hadn't. Then David remembered that he'd written some things about Gene in his diary, such as wondering if Gene was gay. He looked at his stash of diaries in the closet. The diary binders were out of order. So, Gene had probably read the lengthy descriptions of masturbations and related fantasies. David began to wonder if he, David, was the victim.

How stupid not to have hidden the diaries better.

He remembered suddenly that Gene had shown him a pistol he'd bought for protection. With a guy like this running around San Francisco with such missionary ideas of right and wrong, who knew what he was capable of? David wondered if Gene might want to shoot him. *Who's healthier, Gene or me?*

David looked at his calendar. He still had two weeks of vacation left. He surely wasn't going to spend it in stale old San Francisco sleeping in his stale old bed every night, mourning Pem-on-quin and Gene Gatzo. He found his atlas and looked at some of the wide open spaces of California. Once with a friend he'd driven into Baja California and around some of the interesting desert areas of Southern California. He checked a map and noticed that between San Diego and the Salton Sea was a shaded area called Anza-Borrego State Park. It seemed attractive — actual desert, probably without garbage, and not too remote. There were even a few towns in it.

David stood along Highway 86 in Indio, California in warm sunlight, hitchhiking. The air smelled of diesel exhaust. His backpack sat on the candy-wrapper-strewn ground, its zipped-up innards containing his camera, lenses, film, and the essentials — including a pair of panties, not the same ones he took to Gallup.

He remembered the first time he came to California, thumbing all the way from St. Louis, following a vision that he could dress as a woman all the time and live alone in an ocean beach house. As on that trip, the romance of being on the road was quickly fading. Many of those who had picked him up were scruffy and needed gas money. Also, it wasn't easy to walk up to gas station attendants, asking to use rest rooms. Nonetheless, being on his own opened him up and gave him new blood.

When he got out of a salesman's car in Salton City he was close to real desert. The Salton Sea shimmered off in the distance and solitary street signs marked sand-blown, scrubby expanses without homes. David looked at his map and started walking along Highway S-22 into the desert toward the town of Borrego Springs, 30 miles away. He passed a golf course, a temporary splotch of green with surreal old men piloting carts around.

There was plenty of traffic on S-22, mostly old people in big cars not about to pick up a young hitchhiker with beard growth and a backpack. After several hours of walking, his hopes for a ride had turned to sweat in the end-of-the-summer sun and he disgustedly gave up thumbing. *Hell, if I have to walk it, I'll walk it.* At one point he stepped out on an overlook to take a picture of some distant purple-tinted mountains and a black van with dark-tinted bubble windows drove by headed back to the highway. David looked pleadingly toward it but made no attempt to thumb. When the van never slowed down he picked up a pebble and threw it toward its dust cloud.

At mid-afternoon, clouds moved across the sun and things cooled down. David's feet had become intimately acquainted with the irregularities on the bottoms of his boots. Later, at twilight, with little idea of how far he'd come, he was still thumping along on the hard pavement snaking through the desert. He watched the sun retire in a symphony of reds and pinks. In the gathering dusk, David headed down the road toward the light of a distant beacon that pulsed on and off like a friendly firefly. Later, closer, there was barely enough daylight to see that the beacon was at the top of a microwave relay tower several miles away, next to the road. An occasional car still passed, headlights stabbing him briefly.

Darkness had enveloped the area when David's tired legs reached the chain-link fence surrounding the tower. It seemed safe to park his body next to something man-made for the night. He looked up one of the four metal legs of the tower and couldn't see the top because the superstructure receded into the stars of the sky. Only the on-off beacon at the top was visible, merging with the faint lights of high-altitude jets. He shivered and looked anxiously around in the dark. His tired body demanded rest.

He'd been in his sleeping bag next to brush along the fence for only a few minutes when a droplet of moisture hit his cheek. He cussed, then felt several more drops. He hadn't brought a tent or rope, only a flimsy ground cloth. A wind rose, but the rain turned into a fine mist and gradually diminished. David tried to curl into his bag so as to fall asleep but heard an ominous clanking in the tower as though someone was randomly hitting it with a wrench. Finally the reassuring light atop the tower lulled him into a deep sleep.

Sometime later in the bowels of the night he awakened, thinking at first that it was due to the hardness of the ground and that shifting his position would return him to sleep. The tower was still clanking, though not as loudly. As he looked up at it again, the structure seemed weakly illuminated. Then he heard a man's voice. And, in the wind, the sound of an engine idling.

He speculated that some drinking buddies had stopped to consecrate this electronic totem pole and that the light was from their car's headlights. He cautiously listened and waited in his bag to see if the voices would go away. Indeed, the sounds did seem to merge with the night and disappear. Soon the records clerk couldn't be sure if light fell on the tower or not.

Then he heard footsteps and voices, much closer. A light beam methodically began to probe the tower and then the fence. Had he violated the security of this place? When he touched the fence upon arriving had he set off a warning light on someone's cozy control panel hundreds of miles away? He lay still, fantasizing about what would happen if they found him. They'd probably humiliate him and shine lights in his face and tell him to "Get the hell out of here, shithead." He pictured himself refusing to move. Then they would carry him in his sleeping bag and dump him a hundred yards out in the desert. Maybe they'd find his panties in his knapsack and commit unspeakable sexual crimes.

No, he decided, it would be better if he cooperated and pleaded ignorance.

He never really heard anyone drive away. The threatening sounds seemed to merge again with the random noises of the night and he gradually allowed his body to relax. He wasn't about to get up and look around.

The next day, David walked miles more under a cloudy sky. Two miles from Borrego Springs, he got a finally got a lift into town.

The Old Hacienda Motel in Borrego had a nice soft bed which held David as he ate from a grocery bag. For starters, there was pound cake dipped in milk. He lay back and watched TV. At midday there wasn't much on besides an old western with cowboys wearing absurdly-large hats. *Maybe they really did hold ten gallons.*

It was nice to have time to play. He took a dab of hand lotion and smoothed it around his penis, then looked around the motel room. His boots and socks lay strewn around the floor and his clothing was thrown over chairs. He'd have to go to a laundromat to clean up the soiled mess. Rather than dwell on that, he looked at his nude body, so pure-looking after a shower. Hair bushed up from his center like plants growing above a hidden spring.

Now he stroked his penis, which was growing warm and big. As pleasure built he stretched out his long body and briefly felt the residual aches of the long walk.

There was considerable wind outside. He heard something blow against his window — raindrops? Then the front door closed in the adjacent motel room and through an open vent above his door he heard a feminine voice say, "It's raining!" Two car doors slammed and an engine started. David imagined that the woman had come into his room naked, because the voice was naked. He could see her pubic hair and well-formed little cunt and he could imagine his hands grabbing handfuls of ass. He pictured himself lying on his back and her ramming her pussy into his mouth. The tastes would be so repugnant and exciting.

Then the image of Diane took over. He knew he could reach orgasm on that fantasy but put it off. On the TV, which had been distracting to this point, was a department store commercial for a fall and winter sale. A man's voice was saying, "Now you can be whoever you want to be," and on the screen a man quickly changed from cowboy to skier to playboy to motorcycle rider to businessman—by instantly changing clothes.

Really. It's so easy! Almost everyone does drag of some sort. Such great energy!

This was the last place he'd expect to receive a revelation about dressing.

David continued to massage himself slowly. Then a woman appeared on TV advertising a floor mop. She turned to demonstrate and David saw her firm derriere in tight slacks. So perfect. He reached orgasm almost against his will, like a fire hydrant bursting open.

While walking back from a sumptuous dinner at a restaurant that evening he noticed that the wind had risen. He looked toward the west and saw a burgeoning black cloud over nearby mountains. Sand was blowing across the road and sidewalks. Back in his motel room he sat and listened to the howling of the wind, glad like a little boy that he was safe and protected. He excitedly speculated on just how threatening the winds might become.

Turning the TV on seemed sacrilegious at such a moment, so he opened a high-up window through which no one could see him. He undressed completely. Cool air swirled in and around his goose-pimpled body, just as when his father had him naked in the cold basement. His ass clinched tight. The only illumination came from outside the room. He imagined that he was standing with his hands tied behind his back, paying obedience to the goddess of the storm.

His thoughts returned to Diane. He imagined her circling him like a raven, with black, frayed hair and a tattered black dress, her whip stinging his virginal skin in the frigid air.

David opened his eyes, not wanting to pursue that fantasy any longer. He spit in his hand and began to masturbate wildly and fast, standing in the cold. Rubbing his legs tightly together, he imagined them tied with cord. The air seemed to mellow as his juices congregated. The nondescript room took on a pastel hue and the few grains of sand and dust blowing around the room seemed to become grains of sugar. He fixated on the black cloud he'd seen earlier and imagined it to be swirling with faint suggestions of sheer dresses, made-up eyes and jeweled bracelets, and an exotically-costumed belly dancer with an ample, half-erect cock.

He came with sperm melting in his hand.

The next morning he had a dream to record after a night of being safely protected from the wind.

> *I was in the house where I grew up, kind of prowling around. Half of it seemed under construction, with exposed wooden beams at one end. Sunlight shone though the construction, giving the new wood a golden hue. I made my way through crossmembers and support boards into the old part of the house and found the entrance to a secret room I'd always suspected was there. The entrance was dark and I wasn't able to enter.*
>
> *My father, who evidently had been building the new part of the house, came to where I was. He was very proud of his work and contrary to the way I know him, was young, handsome, vibrant and open. He wanted me to take his picture but when I tried, there wasn't enough light and I couldn't.*
>
> *He asked me why I was in this part of the house and I had to make up an excuse because I was aware that inside the secret room were powerful sexual pleasures. I just said I was looking for some books.*

On the outskirts of Borrego Springs, an area of squat houses and crushed-rock yards, a white pickup stopped for David's thumb and took him on a narrow, winding blacktop road up into the rounded mountains where the cloud had been. He got off at a primitive campground whose only amenity was a spring and whose only occupants were two unshaven men sitting next to their camper. Fresh stocked with groceries from town, he struck out into the mountains. He went far enough to get away from the eyes of the men.

He found the terrain a drastic change from the forested Sierra Nevada range to the north. Here was gritty soil, tough thorny bushes, and flaky rock. He noted what life there was — tough, colored lichen attached to boulders, stands of bladed plants that pricked the air, and infrequent dragonflies. Mostly there was stillness. Dead wood lay on the ground. There were no mammals or birds to be seen, only an occasional jet flying speck-high overhead.

David put down his pack and stretched out on a large, flat rock in the warm sun. He wished that he could be all alone in the world to do whatever he wanted — to dress as a woman, or masturbate, or worship the sun — but mainly to experience things purely, without interference.

He stripped down to his stylish and scanty male briefs. Lying in the sun with his hat over his eyes, he imagined that someone looking at him through binoculars would think his body beautiful, maybe arousing. He tried to relax and nap but couldn't because of pesky flies landing on his legs. He idly wondered how long he'd want to stay.

By evening he'd traveled farther from the campground and had located a small space between two huge boulders. He gathered some wood and made a fire at dusk, down in the hollow so that no one could see the flame. Finally he let the fire die, crawled into his sleeping bag and watched the sky for shooting stars before falling asleep. The air had turned cold.

He woke the next morning with relief that he was intact. A distant animal yowled once. The purity of the cool air carrying the sound promised the most intense adventures. He got up quickly and photographed, using the rosy early morning light and color film. At first it seemed there was nothing that personified his feelings — then he became attuned to a huge century plant that had flowered and withered. Candelabra-like pods and tiny crosses adorned its bleached-white stalk. Halfway up the stem a small bird had hollowed out a nest hole. Changing to black and white film, David painstakingly photographed these details. As long as he was photographing he was wonderfully at ease. Then he began to photograph the nearby small mountains as a rising sun illuminated them section by section. They seemed to come to life with distinct personalities.

The sun crept overhead and he became bored again as temperatures and dryness increased—bored with taking pictures, bored with the landscape, bored with himself. He moved on again and found another spot to set up camp. He worried about getting too far from the road—what if anything happened to him? By late afternoon the wind had risen and turned cold again. He sat in the lee of some bushes with his equipment. Thinking that the ultimate reality was himself, he set his camera on a small rock and set the timer to take a self-portrait. The camera slipped off just before the shutter snapped. Cursing, David went over and set it up again. The same thing happened, with more bitter cursing. He assumed his pose one more time, next to his backpack, and the camera finally behaved.

He wondered whether anyone looking at the photo would know he was sucking on three prunes in his mouth. *Maybe this photo will be the last evidence of me. Maybe I'll die and animals will eat me. The only things left would be my bones, my pictures and my diary.*

He doubted that anyone would even go to the bother of getting the pictures developed. Or if they did, they'd take them to a drug store and get small, grayish prints back. He realized, sitting there grim and stone-still in the breeze, that he had a powerful desire to be remembered.

He realized that if he died in this desolate, moon-like landscape no one in California would miss him at all. If he didn't show up for work he'd make the AWOL list and bureaucratic wheels would only slowly begin to turn. No one who knew him knew where he was. Only the people he'd hitchhiked with and the two guys in the campground had had any contact with him. Well, he *had* registered in the motel down in Borrego Springs.

Gene Gatzo probably didn't care any more. There was just family, mostly in Ohio—those distant brothers and sisters and parents who sent birthday and Christmas presents every year out of habit. They might care if he died. They might make some ceremony for him and remember him if he died. Of course he would still be a mystery to them, having flown the roost to go to California.

He chuckled. *Why all this stuff about death? I'm out here by my own choice. I'm grown up and free, and I've taken the paths that seemed right for me.* David began to blame himself for not having become the photographer he wanted to be. If only he'd exerted himself and taken himself seriously. That was it—he'd never taken himself seriously. He played at things like he played with himself.

He looked at his nearly-empty canteens and knew that in the morning he'd have to return to the campground to get water. It wasn't dark yet but the air was getting frigid, so he slid into his sleeping bag and found a comfortable spot. He fell asleep briefly, and when he woke, stars were beginning to come out, bright and crisp in the deepening blue-black sky. He looked at familiar constellations. The sky turned black.

David felt himself lying at the bottom of an immense stellar pool. He was part of a vast space, yet the stars seemed close enough to touch. As he gave himself over to euphoria and lost track of time, he began to float somewhere up above his body. The feeling, as his kernel of consciousness seemed to grow and expand without limit, suddenly made him stop short and grab for something to hold on to—his body. *Oh my God, I was on the verge of something.*

Back on earth again, he was aware of lying on rocky, uneven ground with cold night air on his face. He reached out to his pack, found water to drink and opened a package of cookies. The voraciousness with which he gulped one down surprised him. The cookie was cold and stiff, yet David had eaten it as though it was his last meal, like a baby noisily sucking at its mother's breast.

Two salty tears rolled down his cheeks and wet the cool nylon of his sleeping bag. His stomach seemed to drop out of him. The thought that he was crying made him cry more. The whole stupid thrust of the last year became apparent—the crime of half-ass relationships and wasting his life in a job he didn't like.

David threw the package of cookies out into the night. To think that he'd started crying because of the way he'd eaten a goddamn cookie! Everything seemed wrong. He wanted to go back home. The dark night frightened him. It was as though he'd offended some huge giant who would come along and stomp on him.

Before returning to sleep he pulled the pair of panties from his knapsack, slipped them on inside the sleeping bag and slept with his hand between his legs.

At two o'clock the next afternoon he was on the road hitchhiking. He got as far as Long Beach before dark. After the purity of the mountains, the complexity and savageness of the city shocked him. He looked at the first newspaper in a week and saw stories of California murders and body counts in Viet Nam.

Still, he had warm feelings about the pictures he'd taken in the desert.

13

Upon returning home David hoped to maintain his momentum, but he knew the glow would last only a few days.

There was a letter under the door of his apartment. He expected another lecture from Gene but found instead a business letter announcing the apartment building's sale and a rent increase of $120. David snorted with indignation. How dare they? The building had been family-owned, with the owners living only a few blocks away. If he locked himself out, a quick call brought them over in minutes to let him in. It was likely that a speculator bought the building because the letter said to send the rent to a realty office. David resolved to move.

He decided that the rent increase would be a godsend. This workaday and dull neighborhood had never brought him much joy. Every day he saw the same old man walk to the corner store to get his daily bag of groceries. Teenagers were out at all hours on weekends banging on their cars. He needed a change, a new space, and more exciting surroundings. Living in the Excelsior

District had been lonely, tinged with the morbid.

In the last few days before his return to work, and Gene Gatzo, David toiled in his kitchen darkroom developing film from the trip. The pictures of the century plant seemed superb. His renditions of the play of sunlight and shadow on boulders were exactly as he'd planned. He marked the best frames on his contact sheets and put them aside.

The first thing he noticed at the office was that Gene was nowhere in sight. The ladies were busy with their desk work and didn't seem to pay David any special attention, so evidently Gene hadn't told anyone. Maybe everyone was giving him the silent treatment.

Trying to act casual, but finding himself with a slight Gatzo-like stutter, David asked The Jock where Gene was.

The Jock leaned back. "Yeah, Dave. You've been on vacation, haven't you? You haven't heard."

"Heard what?"

The Jock paused to lend emphasis to his words. "You won't believe this. Our friend got himself in a bunch of trouble."

David waited until The Jock returned with a clipping one of the office women had been keeping.

SHOT WITH OWN GUN

A Veteran's Administration employee was shot with his own pistol last night as he returned to his downtown San Francisco hotel.

Eugene J. Gatzo, 26, a resident of the Hotel Astrid, 725 O'Farrell St., reported being accosted by four youths. According to the victim, the youths attempted to mug him, and when he drew his pistol, a fight for the weapon ensued. During the scuffle, the gun discharged and a bullet entered Gatzo's leg. Police were unable to find the suspects or the weapon.

Gatzo is in stable condition at Kaiser Hospital.

David inquired about Gene's condition.

"He'll be OK—just went through his thigh muscle. He'll have to walk with a crutch or cane for a while."

"When's he coming back?"

"A week or so. Are you going to see him in the hospital?"

"I guess I'd better."

"I mean, you guys are pretty good friends, aren't you?"

"Oh, yeah. We've done some things together." David hoped The Jock didn't think there was more to him and Gene than friendship, though The Jock was always making off-color remarks about coworkers. "I guess it'd be the right thing to go see him."

The Jock leaned back in his chair and smiled. "What'd'ya do on your vacation?"

"I was in Arizona and New Mexico—then down in the desert near San Diego for awhile."

The Jock pretended to raise a camera to his eyes and click off a shot. "Shutterbugging as usual?"

David detested that word. "I'm always taking pictures. You know me."

The Jock described how he and Vince and one of the office women had gone to see Gene the day following the shooting. "He said some Asian kids did it. If you want my opinion, I don't even think they were trying to rob him, they were just playing with him. He must've said something that ticked them off."

"His having a gun was a mistake."

"Yeah, right. Oh, say, I didn't know he was staying at your place before he moved to the hotel."

How much did The Jock know? "I told him he could stay there while I was on vacation. He kind of left things in a mess."

"That's funny, he said *you* were messy."

With exceptional luck, David found an attractive, traditional Victorian flat just after the landlord posted the FOR RENT sign. This was an apartment with character, offering a tiny ornamental fireplace, high ceilings, rich woodwork, a slightly-sagging back porch where a darkroom could be installed, and a back yard with shade trees and garden possibilities. It was on Hancock Street near the gay Castro district of town, and it was only natural that the upstairs flat was occupied by a gay couple. David could barely afford it, having to pay first and last month's rent and a deposit. He figured the only way to keep the place and still live decently would be to have a paying roommate.

When he moved in and began to re-paint the interior during the wee hours of the night, he thought that a roommate might be just what he needed. It was time for him to draw out of his shell and get rid of lingering memories of Diane.

A week after he finished moving in, he ran an ad in the *Bay Guardian* asking for a female roommate. He received several calls from women, but none came to see the place. With his savings low he resorted to running an ad for roommates of either sex. Then the respondents were all men. David was reluctantly about to choose between three straight guys when he got a call from Jeanette, the woman he'd talked with at the Pacific Images party. Inviting him to an opening of a textile art display, she promised that the catering company she worked for would be supplying "beaucoup good food" and that he should attend if only for the feast.

David expressed interest, then went on to describe his new place.

"Do you need a roommate?"

"Yeah, why? Do you know someone who's looking?"

"Am I glad I called. Let me put it this way. I've been living with Brian for two years. You met him, didn't you?"

"I think so."

"Well, to put it simply, we're not getting along any more. He just gets in moods and closes off. I've decided to leave. It's not working any more. So, I'm looking for a place. Can I come over and see what you've got?"

David fended off the male hopefuls for a few more days until the tall Jeanette could visit. David guessed her age as 24. She came on a Saturday afternoon with flashing eyes and big red lips like an excited kid. David showed her the two rooms set aside for a roommate and the rest of the long apartment, proud of the freshly-painted white walls. As he walked with her, he kept noticing her generous hips and bosom, and her blonde, bushy hair.

"Well, what do you think?"

"I really, really love it. It's a great part of town and I've got friends nearby. So, in 20 words or less, David, I'd like to share this place with you. Say OK, OK?"

They sat down to talk business. Her finances were slim because she only worked part-time for the catering service. Her artistic efforts—the weaving—were only paying for the materials. "But I live very simply," she said, as though the right word from him would cascade a shower of lucky magic on her.

"Would Brian still be seeing you here?"

"I think we've split for good. He's leaving for Idaho."

As he'd done with the previous interested men, David explained that he was a TV. "You should know in advance."

"Then you're gay?"

"No, no. There are a lot of hetero TVs. But really, what I need to know is if my dressing up once in awhile would bother you."

"I don't know. How often do you do this?"

David tried to talk nonchalantly, as though they were talking about someone else. "Every month to go to a meeting up the street—we have a society for transvestites. Occasionally I dress up here at home so I can take pictures of myself."

"This is really something. I've never known anyone into this. I guess it'd be OK."

They went to see the two empty rooms again. David could see Jeanette's eyes already deciding where things should go. Before she left, he promised to make up his mind soon about a roommate. He spied on her through the front window as she walked away, book bag slung over her shoulder. *She's nice, she's into art and she doesn't have a man.*

He talked to one more woman about the apartment that afternoon, a photographer who'd noticed he listed a darkroom in his ad. A thin, driven woman, she too fell in love with the flat and eyed the darkroom space. When he mentioned he was a TV she quickly made excuses and left.

After calling with the good news, David helped Jeanette move in, using the catering company's van. It was true that she didn't have much—her loom, a hunk of foam on the floor for a mattress, two suitcases of clothes and an aging VW bug. The little trinkets and mementos she brought seemed precious and religious. In many cases, she explained, they were gifts from other artists or admirers. Like David, she kept diaries.

That evening when he was cooking a simple meal for the two of them and feeling brotherly he found himself saying magnanimously that they should just stay roommates and not make any sexual overtures. She wholeheartedly agreed. They would be best friends, she said. Later at work David thought about how nice it would be to come home and have a woman in the house to talk to. They were both artists, he with his photography and her with her weaving. The arrangement could only be positive for them. On the other hand, there was always the chance that she'd fall for him . . .

They walked up a trail from Muir Woods basin toward the top of Mt. Tam. It was a warm and sunny Sunday, the first chance they'd had to do something together outside. Jeanette seemed refreshed and sure of herself since the split from Brian. They were in a redwood grove and the light filtering down provided a relaxing tableau. She watched as David jumped to the far side of a stream. He crouched down and focused his camera on a miniature waterfall, totally absorbed.

Later she lay atop a large, flat rock in the sun. David joined her, stretching out and baring his chest. Their hands were only inches apart, and he wanted to touch her, but they just lay there basking, semi-sleeping, until a Boy Scout troop came up the trail.

Later, nearby, David took pictures of her standing in a shaft of sunlight with her eyes closed. She certainly wasn't a Raquel Welch, but her confidence and natural sensuality was making his heart race. Why, he wondered, did he have to fall for every woman who came his way?

When her friend Rod came the next night David tried to act blasé. The unshaven man she introduced as a Berkeley poet seemed out of place against the stark, shiny hardwood floors of the flat. He seemed like a refugee from the streets — a bum, practically. Jeanette's flushed and excited face said it all. David retreated to his darkroom rather than sit around straining to hear what they were doing in her room. He had decided to try for a show of his desert photographs and had begun making large black and white prints.

When he finished his work around midnight, Jeanette's room at the front of the house was dark and quiet. There was just the sound of his print washer swooshing water methodically around soggy photographs. He hadn't been able to remove Jeanette entirely from his mind. That scruffy man was up there, David was sure, sleeping with her in David's own house! As he poured his used chemicals into storage bottles he remembered ruefully the time he'd stopped to pick up a good-looking woman hitchhiker when he'd had a car. After she negotiated a ride and started to get in, her boyfriend and a big white dog appeared from behind a bush and joined her.

Eventually David felt comfortable enough to try to call Gene at the hospital. After all, he would have to work with him again. Gene answered from his extension. He sounded older and a bit shaky.

"Say, Gene, this is David from work."

There was a moment of silence. "Yeah?"

"I—I'm calling to see how you are. Sorry to hear about what happened."

"Well, they say they're going to r-release me by the weekend. I had some complications." Gene went on to describe some of the nurses and orderlies on a first-name basis.

"Say, ah . . . I'd like to come by and say hello if that's OK."

Gene wasn't enthusiastic but they set a time. An hour later he called back. "I-I thought it over. I-It wouldn't be good. I'd just get upset."

He has some nerve. Getting hurt makes him think he's a big shot. So Gene-boy doesn't want to be upset.

On the other hand, maybe the shooting had in some way made Gene wiser. David pictured him lying in his hospital bed taking stock of his life.

Jeanette was out of the apartment working on the catering of an evening party. David was alone and wearing a filled-out bra while working in the darkroom. He hadn't worn any of his women's clothing yet in Jeanette's presence because he thought it might compromise him. So he received a major jolt when he walked into the kitchen and saw her at the table munching carrots and reading. He had on a loose sweater and hoped that she hadn't noticed. Breezing through as though in a hurry, David spoke as he looked through negative files in the next room.

"You're back early."

"They didn't need me to serve. I just helped put the food together."

"I suppose you would've liked to work the longer hours."

"No, not really, I was tired. Besides, I've made enough money this month. Gives me more time on the loom." She resumed crunching carrots.

He wished that she'd go to her room so she'd be out of his hair. He could, of course, sneak off to the bedroom and take off the bra, but he didn't want to hide in his own house. So he walked back into the kitchen with his contact sheet and negatives and sat down across from Jeanette. Her eyes went first to his face then to his chest.

She didn't seem perturbed. "I thought that you just dressed up all the way. But you like to go around with just a bra on? If I have friends over it'd look kind of weird."

"Well, I like to do this in private. I didn't expect you to be here!" He caught himself before he became too apologetic. "Sometimes I wear panties under my trousers. Even to work. I've got quite a collection of pretty things."

She didn't indicate a burning desire to see them. "Why do you wear these things? I mean, to me they're just things I wear every day. There's no thrill to it. Sometimes wearing a bra all day can be pretty uncomfortable."

David leaned back in his chair, cradling his breasts with his crossed arms, and looked out the window. Logically explaining it took the fun away. Putting things into words was like trying to make it into something wholesome. He continued anyway, comparing men's underwear to women's.

Jeanette giggled, then resumed her serene moon-Madonna face again. "Yes, but I wear these things every day, you know. They don't *move* me like they seem to move you."

"Well, it's funny. Sometimes I just like to wear the stuff. Some other times I really get off on it. Fetishes, you know. I have some very hot masturbations wearing your sort of things."

Jeanette blushed and looked away, rolling her eyes slightly and sighing as if to say, "How did I get myself into this?"

David hoped that he hadn't killed his chances with these disclosures. On the other hand, even if they never made it at least he was opening some freedom for himself. He wondered if he would ever be comfortable walking around the house totally dressed in her presence. He thought that he might try it, just to make a point. To show her that . . . he didn't need her?

Jeanette left for work at five on a still-dark morning. David rose ten minutes after the front door closed and went to her room, listening for any sign of her unexpected return. He detected delightfully distinctive smells there—faint perfumes, a slight mustiness, body odor from her unmade bed, and the honey-like sweetness of cut flowers. When he went to her dresser and pulled out the top drawer, a new host of fragrances played upon his senses. What was it that women used to make their underwear so provocatively pungent?

David experienced a déjà vu of the highest order, remembering similarly being in his parents' room as a fifteen-year-old, violating his mother's lingerie drawer, feeling the sensual nylon, satin and elastic of her private things.

Running his hands magically through Jeanette's bras and panties was like touching parts of her. Another part of him calmly rated her level of taste, which was better than average. He would know—he'd been through many other women's drawers in his time. Jeanette had some slinky red panties, low cut, and some black lace creations. David wondered which ones she wore for Rod.

After making a thorough reconnaissance of her closet—not as exciting as the drawer—he borrowed the sexiest things, along with a pair of her leather boots, and took them to his room. He undressed hastily and pulled on her tight black panties. Lying down, he put one of her boots between his legs so that the shiny heel protruded into him. His eventual orgasm was high up on the Richter Scale.

As he'd learned to do as a teenager, he replaced everything in its exact place before he left for work. He felt vaguely guilty. It was like having sex with her spirit, the spirit that stayed behind in her clothing. *Maybe I can't deal with the whole of her. Maybe I'm just a ghost-fucker.*

He had to tell The Jock at work eventually. Yes, I have a female roommate. No, we're not lovers. Yes, she turns me on. No, I haven't gone to bed with her. Well, I value the relationship and I don't want to scare her away.

Barring his mother and sister, he'd never lived with a woman for the length of time he'd been with Jeanette. He'd never had to divide chores before. There were the all-important questions of who would do the dishes and take out the garbage, of who would pay the bills and who would sweep and vacuum. The volume level of the TV had to be negotiated. Would they share this meal or that? She taught him that it wasn't nice to leave whiskers around the quaint old bathroom sink they shared, nor a ring around the four-footed bathtub.

The VA clerk began to consider his relationship a sixty per cent one. If her boyfriend, and she had taken on a new one since Rod, had her for an occasional evening or day, David had her for a much longer time. David grudgingly came around to respect the boundary between them.

He took many admiring photos of her. He told her several times that he loved her and this embarrassed her. Sometimes they talked about their plans. David admitted that he'd eventually like to get married, "as crazy as that sounds." She wanted to get married too, "but I've got some living to do first."

14

David-as-Natalie walked into a gay bar on outer Market Street one night, recognizing some Diana Society regulars in the hazy, dim light. She had walked a scary five blocks from her flat to The Parlour, where the Society had begun holding nighttime get-togethers. The Parlour also included a straight restaurant.

Natalie hadn't been sure, walking along Church Street under streetlights, if passers-by had seen through her. If they had, they'd been polite and didn't stare. She had worn an unremarkable coat that took away the thrust of her breasts and covered her face slightly with a large collar. It had been a thrill to pass by men who had sex in their eyes—to see them from the eyes of a woman.

If anything gave her away, she thought, it was her not-quite convincing gait, so she tried walking with smaller steps.

"Natalie!" exclaimed Karen, using a pay phone in a shadowy corner of the bar. She walked over and they warmly embraced. Karen's body felt good. The doctor was wearing a wraparound dress which displayed her figure well.

"My dear, you do look ravishing," said Karen, noticing Natalie's improved confidence.

"Well, babe, let's party tonight!" said Natalie. "I've had a tough week at the office."

With glasses of wine from a beefy, quite gay bartender, and hors d'oeuvres, Karen and Natalie made their way through knots of other TVs, some of whom provided amusement to the bar regulars with their unkempt wigs over weathered old men's faces. Sitting down at the one remaining empty table, Karen was eager to talk. She whispered, "I've started taking hormone shots. I've been seeing Doctor Phil, you know, Doctor Samuelson."

After a startled look from Natalie, Karen continued. "I think I eventually want to have the operation. But while my buds are developing I'll have lots of time to think about it. Jean wishes I wouldn't. But it seems right. I'd really like to live as a female all the time."

"You'd make a beautiful woman," said Natalie, speaking softly. "But remember, once you've done it there's no turning back—that's it." Natalie made a karate chop on the table. "No dickie no more, forever. Besides, what would it do to your practice? Parents would worry about bad influences on their kids."

Karen only smiled. "You *know* I've thought about all that. But what it comes down to is that you only go around this merry-go-round once and we might as well do it the way that suits us best—that's a pun, dear. I'm happy to say that I've saved a tidy sum over the years so I can afford to lose some of my patients for awhile. Who knows? I might even relocate."

Somehow Karen had seemed too lighthearted to have conscientiously put money away.

Karen winked. "Don't tell me you haven't thought about a sex change."

"I hate operations. I really do! Actually, I thought about it a couple times. But I'm the first to admit that I have a lousy figure and a man's face. I know I wouldn't look good as a woman. You're lucky, you have such a classy face."

Karen smiled.

"But really," Natalie continued, "I wouldn't like the idea of having a nice part of me cut off. I just like the idea of being able to change from one sex to another whenever I want. And last but

114

not least I might want to be a father some day."

"Freeze some sperm."

"Yeah, and what happens if someone pulls the plug? Seriously, having a sex change isn't a possibility here."

They both became distracted by a woman visitor with a good-looking boyfriend in tow. Everything—her manner, voice, dress and looks—said *woman*, the sort men compete for. She soon let on that she'd had a sex change. As she virtually held court among the admiring TVs, Karen looked on with awe and jealousy. Later, the two talked.

The party had become increasingly lively. Natalie had never been so relaxed while dressed and acting the part. She felt she could drop her guard and have fun rather than worrying about displaying masculine traits. When two tipsy straight businessmen blundered into the bar and tried to pick her and Karen up, Natalie knew how far she'd come.

When closeted, she used to concentrate on such refined delights as how lingerie felt against her skin. Now the thrill was in the finer points of makeup and in passing in public. The Diana Society's occasional classes helped.

In October David decided to dress up as a cowgirl and go to the Hookers' Ball. On the appropriate Saturday evening he showered and put on his padded girdle and very tight blue jeans. There was no hint of a penis behind the zipper. He wore rented chaps, borrowed cowboy boots and a very white, close-fitted shirt over his bra. A sheriff's badge and cowboy hat over a curly blond wig completed the fantasy. Seeing that his costume was in a playful vein, Jeanette helped out, arranging David's wig and offering suggestions on his makeup. When they finished he had her photograph him in various amusing poses. "This is fun," she allowed.

"You should go with me sometime."

"Are you going to any other balls?"

"A week from today."

"What as?"

"I'll be in an evening gown."

"Where's the ball?"

"The Hyatt at Embarcadero Center. You could go as a giant

bumble bee."

"You're reading my mind, David. But no, not as a bee. I think I'd like to go, but I think I'll surprise you." She gave him a rare coquettish smile.

David-as-Natalie got a lift to the Civic Auditorium for the Hookers' Ball with Karen and two other Society members. Karen, dressed in a fifties prom dress with built-up bosom, tight waist and fluffed-out skirt, sat beside Natalie in the back seat of a small car. Karen's hand snuck between Natalie's legs against the roughness of her Levi's. The two then over-dramatically kissed while a beautiful Asian TV in the front seat tisk-tisked and shook her head in mock disapproval.

Natalie had known they were moving toward this moment. The kiss was fun, yet mixed with the forbidden and unnatural, because behind Karen's sexy lipstick and eye shadow and dress were male muscles and a trace of beard. Natalie was aroused—and queasy.

Natalie had her camera and flash as always and shot two rolls of celebrants at the ball. Some of the men wore scanty G-strings while more than a few women displayed their breasts. Toward the end, when he took a series of photos of a walking banana, there were plenty of volunteers to join in the pictures.

After the party, with unresolved energy between her legs, David-as-Natalie went home and developed the film. There were some solid, exciting shots. The following Monday he stopped by Pacific Image, the stock photo agency, to leave some other prints for their files. Sam Waggoner was there, working busily at her desk while baby-sitting her sister's three-year-old. This time Sam's muumuu was a wild flower print. Eventually, she offhandedly asked if he had any shots of "wildness in San Francisco. You know, outrageous costumes, general licentiousness."

"Funny you should bring that up. It seems like that's all I've been shooting lately."

"Well, whatever moves you. *TIME* called and they're going to do major coverage about new American ways of having fun. They want some interesting stuff on how far we go out here."

"Hmmm. I have lots of black and white material. Is that OK for them?" He tried to act as though dealing with *TIME* would be just another business transaction.

Sam shook her head and explained that *TIME* used mostly

color. She allowed that he might bring in some transparencies "and a few of the best black-and-whites" from the Beaux Artes Ball he was attending with Jeanette. "Also, there might be a tie-in with TIME-LIFE books."

"By the way, I like the prints you left here last time. I'd suggest giving your prints more contrast in the future, though."

David felt humbled as he shuffled down the worn wooden steps to the street. He concluded that she must badger all of her photographers this way.

At home, he found another letter from his mother in the mailbox.

> *Dear David,*
>
> *I want to think you for your letter. It made me feel so good to think that you cared to write.*
>
> *I think that your father is trying to understand you. There was a program on PBS recently and I kind of "arranged" for him to be watching TV when it came on. A part of it was about what you are. He almost switched the channel at first, but the film was pretty non-controversial and he ended up watching it all. At least we know more now about different lifestyles.*
>
> *Sometimes your father and I think back about raising you kids in a small town and wonder if that was right. You grew up in an isolated atmosphere.*
>
> *You said in your letter that you were dressing up when you were living with us as a teenager. It makes us feel bad (well, me mostly) that you had to keep it from us. Of course, we probably would've tried to discourage you from doing it. As I said, we didn't know about people doing those things.*
>
> *Well, I've gone on long enough. I finally showed your last letter to your father and I guess he coped. Sometimes I think he hates things to get complicated.*
>
> *We'd like you to write again if you could.*
>
> *Love, Mom and Dad*

David poked through the dress racks at the Friends of the Ballet thrift store on outer California Street looking for a dress to wear to the Beaux Artes Ball. He was the only man in the women's section and he thought his purpose must be transparent. It was too bad, he thought, that he was larger than the average woman. He usually took a size sixteen dress. The sexy ones were usually a size twelve or fourteen. All he could find in sixteen were absurdly cut, dismally plain ones. Except for the one he had just uncovered. He ran the black velvet material between his fingers. The bodice was low-cut and classically simple.

He took the dress to a seamstress favored by some Diana Society members. The woman was quite busy with work for other TVs and complained that she had no time until after the ball season. David managed to get on her good side and finally she agreed to help, saying that she'd rather fit a dress to a TV who wasn't overweight.

Fortunately, they agreed, the dress had been floor-length, so it wouldn't be too short when altered for him. When David showed up for the first fitting two days later the woman again complained that she didn't have enough time and nobody appreciated her. Finally she threw her head back in exasperation and began to pin the dress on him, making chalk marks as she went. She said he had chosen well—the dress would look good on him.

All this took place in a back room of her storefront, concealed from her straight customers.

On the night of the ball David could barely contain himself. Jeanette was dressing in her candle-lit room as a butterfly. She'd made her wings and mask of papier-mâché and had painted the whole outfit violet and purple. In the bathroom, David shaved the parts of his body which would show, then began a process of taping his chest to imitate the beginnings of breasts above his dress's bodice. Because his skin wasn't loose, the taping hurt a little. Filling out the cups of his bra were cloth sacks of rice. Finally, on went the dress. David-as-Natalie felt as tight as the rigging on a clipper ship and as loose as a slinky black panther.

After final touchups to her makeup and long, blond wig that shone in the light, Natalie lifted her new high heels to appreciate them. Admiring herself in the mirror, she dabbed a touch of per-

fume to her neck and to her thigh, vaguely hoping it might bring
luck. For a moment she imagined David meeting Natalie on the
street—surely he'd be captivated!

Wobbling slightly on her slender heels, she traipsed down
the hall and found Jeanette on the phone in her room. When Natalie bent over and kissed her neck, Jeanette looked around,
speechless.

They parked Jeanette's VW in one of the cavernous Embarcadero Center garages, then Natalie escorted Jeanette like an older sister might across the street to the Hyatt Regency. They circulated for a time in the ballroom lobby looking at all the sinful,
Marti Gras-like costumes. Natalie took photos of men in leather,
lingerie or full drag and of real women dressed fancifully. Then
sexy, pounding, disco-style music drew the pair into the ballroom. Through a smoky haze and the crush and warmth of beautiful bodies they entered an immense area with mirrored ceilings
and columns and sat at one of the round tables the Diana Society
had reserved.

As Jeanette saw the show that underground San Francisco
was capable of her eyes grew larger every minute.

Finally the official show began—the judging of costumes for
individuals and groups. Natalie self-consciously made her way
up to the stage to take photographs. Straight newspaper photographers, several of whom Natalie recognized from her riot-
photography days, made room for her without recognizing her.
On the stage above were processions of costumes overflowing
with feathers, gold and silver. Like cut flowers, the costumes
would be used only this one time.

After a few glasses of wine Natalie became more gregarious.
Costumed celebrants circulating below the stage seemed at ease
being photographed by her because she was one of them. Some
propositioned her and gay men put their arms around her. It was
a night where even dirty old men could do almost anything they
wanted.

The show seemed to go on forever. Groups paraded on stage
with Egyptian or Oriental themes. Some had an outer space mo-
tif. Just when the audience thought a production had climaxed, as
in a fireworks display, a final surprise would bring gasps and

cheers.

Natalie drank in the atmosphere of magic and conjuration. For one night she could leave the world of dullness and conformity. Here the blossoming of imagination and goodwill prevailed.

15

Despite her good spirits, Natalie fretted about the quality of her photography at the Beaux Artes Ball. A new spot meter helped remove some of the uncertainty about exposures. Still, she kept rechecking the settings on her camera, concerned she might be using the wrong shutter speeds or f-stops. Also, the flash seemed to take forever to charge—why hadn't she remembered to take extra batteries?

Natalie suddenly remembered she'd promised to take table shots of Society members for the club newsletter. This wasn't a job she looked forward to—there were too many TVs and their friends and it would be difficult to attract their attention. Still, she diligently set out to do just that.

When she started by photographing her own table she was happy to see that Jeanette, while retaining a certain reserve, was talking to nearby TVs. At the next table, Natalie didn't particularly notice a person in a black tux who smiled obligingly along with the others when the black-velveted photographer's flash went off.

Natalie, her clothes in temporary disarray, sat in a cubicle in the women's restroom. She had finally given in to nature's call, put off for an hour.

When coming in, she'd passed some curvaceous young women in the powder room dressed in tight cat costumes. Seeming to like the idea of men dressed as women, one had flirtatiously suggested she might accompany Natalie into a cubicle. Her friends had giggled and Natalie had smiled her best "I'm flattered" smile.

After getting herself rigged up again, and feeling pain from having her chest taped up so long, Natalie admired herself in the mirror next to the cat-women before sailing out again into the swirl. She dodged the glare of television lights and a reporter interviewing Mayor Moscone.

As Natalie walked back to her table, tipsily talking to herself, she rounded a large mirrored column and almost bumped into a tall person in a black tuxedo who said "Hi" in a decidedly female voice. Screeching to a halt, expecting to see someone she knew, Natalie saw a woman with brown eyes and hair pulled back masculinely into a bun. A large black bow tie, red carnation, white gloves and silver cuff links completed the effect.

"We haven't been introduced," said the woman pleasantly. "I think you photographed our table?"

Natalie was preoccupied with the woman's face. There was a certain comeliness and reserved humor there. It was the face of a woman who'd been in the outdoors, a face touched by the wind and sun, yet one that didn't tan easily. An English face.

Natalie suspected that the person wanted a print of her group photo. "Yes, that would've been me. I'm playing society photographer tonight."

"You look like a person I'd like to know. I haven't seen you at any Diana Society parties before." The woman's directness was disconcerting.

"I'm a recent, ah, member, should I say? But then I've been to meetings lately and haven't seen you." Something made Natalie want to reach out and touch the woman's earlobe and its tiny jeweled earring.

"I just go to the splashy things a few times a year with my

friends from Palo Alto. But you, what is your name? . . . Natalie. Perfect. You've made yourself into quite a beautiful woman. Do you know how sexy you look?"

"No. I mean, thank you. I do feel nice tonight. A little wine, liberated people, neat things to take pictures of." Natalie began telling the story of how she'd found her dress, then remembered she didn't know the first thing about this woman.

"Patricia. Call me Pat."

"A nice unisexual name."

"Thank you."

"I'm admiring *your* outfit. Very spiffy. Very polished. Believe it or not, I've never worn a tux."

"Well, you should sometime."

Natalie was embarrassingly out of words. This sort of thing hadn't been in the script. Besides, maybe this woman was just toying with her—what if she found out how dull the David part of her was?

"Do you dance?" asked Pat.

Natalie allowed Pat to take her arm as they walked out to the dance floor. They lucked into a slow tune and the two held each other closely. Natalie inhaled the beguiling scent of Pat's perfume. She half expected to feel the hardness of a man's body but instead felt the muted softness of breasts. Her hands detected the swelling of hips. She knew that if they danced this closely all evening and didn't go further, she would be a very frustrated girl-boy.

They danced the better part of an hour. Natalie mentioned that she thought she was a real-life Cinderella and that everyone must be looking at them. Then, her lips touching a soft wisp of Pat's hair, she dared whisper that "A certain part of me wishes it could get free."

"Could it be that you are interested in me?" Pat asked softly in Natalie's ear.

"That's an understatement."

"We-l-l-l-l, we could go upstairs—before you turn back into a pumpkin." Patricia let it be known that she and several of her Diana Society friends had rented a suite in the hotel for the evening.

"That's lovely. But what do you propose to do if we go there? I mean, we've just met. Surely you don't expect—"

"Oh, hell, just come on up for a few drinks. Hey, you can trust me! I wouldn't do anything you wouldn't." Pat deepened her voice.

"OK, then. But we can't get my dress mussed," Natalie insisted as they left the dance floor.

Natalie walked quickly over to Jeanette, realizing with a start that she'd completely forgotten about her photo gear. *That* rarely if ever happened. Jeanette was sitting alone at the table looking sleepy.

"Jeanette! I'm sorry I've left you alone for so long, I really am. What's happened is that I've met someone and I suspect that we'll spend the night here in the hotel."

Jeanette smiled sweetly. "I saw you dancing. You looked really nice together."

Natalie had hoped that Jeanette would be jealous. "Jeanette Butterfly," Natalie said, bending over so as to brush her roommate's shoulder with her hair, "can you drive home by yourself and take the camera stuff too?"

"Of course. Have a good time," winked Jeanette.

Just then Pat joined them and was properly introduced. Next to Jeanette, Pat seemed so much more grown-up and mature. As they left, Natalie glanced back and saw Jeanette casting a confused look at them.

Gleaming escalators carried the hand-holding couple up into the hotel's main lobby. After the revelry in the ballroom, the mostly straight world above was like moving from Jamaica to Billings. Natalie felt tourists' glances, though the confidence emanating from Patricia helped. The two entered a glassed-in elevator along with an inebriated, over-the-hill straight couple who seemed to know what was happening.

"We must look OK," Natalie said after they stepped out on the proper floor. They paused to look down into the spacious courtyard with its massive globe floating on a pool of water. Trees held cages of doves whose faint coos melted into the air. Nearby, bored hotel guests lounged, waiting for unforeseen events to occur in their lives.

For the first time since leaving the protective atmosphere of the ball, Natalie relaxed. Part of her enjoyed the tightness of her garments and the security of being confined. She liked the perfume in her hair. Another part of her felt just a little silly, as though she was a little boy again in a grade school play. *What I'd like most now is some sex, just some nice warm cozy sex.*

Patricia's suite consisted of two rooms. After mixing drinks in the first, they proceeded into the softly-lit second room and locked the door. Pat opened a window and let some cool night air in while David-as-Natalie came over and peered out at the lights of the city. The sounds he heard and the complexity of buildings and traffic made him think the entire city was pulsing with energy from the ball.

Pat lay on one of the beds quietly looking at David. She called for him in a soft way, the way a mother might call for a child at bedtime.

David turned from his reverie, realizing guiltily that he'd lost some steam. At first, Pat's newness and exoticness had overwhelmed him — their first touches had seemed nearly as potent as orgasms. Now David felt more like burying his head in the breasts she had exposed. He lay down next to her and gave in to her desire to play.

They held each other tightly. In David's stomach was a sugar-water and vinegar mixture of dread and excitement. Pat's kiss seemed too soft, too mushy.

Pat pulled up David's dress and ran her hand up his thighs to the center of his tight padded girdle. David stood up, self-consciously pulled off the girdle and exposed his cock, which had been buried for too long. Then David looked at Pat's breasts under her suspenders and his prick came to life, a snake-puppy in folds of velvet.

Pat's female shape emerging from her male clothing disappointed David somewhat. He preferred a slender, more male-like body with smaller breasts. Her hips were too wide. But Pat seemed experienced and responsive. Her hands knew where to touch. When poised over her, he looked down at his own breasts and nyloned legs and felt his long hair falling past his face and onto hers. He was glowing.

16

For days, David had been checking the convenience store at the VA building for the arrival of the latest *TIME* magazine. Then, there it was. On the cover was a breaking news story about an oil spill along the coast of France. There was absolutely nothing in the issue about Having Fun In America.

Sam Waggoner told him to be patient about the photos from the Beaux Artes Ball she'd submitted to *TIME*.

A week later David was again hanging around the store. The salesclerk said the magazine was late. Towards the end of the workday, David snuck out of the office to look for the magazine. Finally, there it was, with a bright, brassy cover and the headline *Having Fun in the 70s — Leisure-Time America*.

He quickly flipped pages to find the article, but saw none of his pictures. The photos were by *TIME* staffers or from big photo agencies. He disparagingly paged on through the third and fourth pages of the layout. *Shit*. Then on the last page of the spread he saw — as his heart skipped two beats — one of his black and white photos of TVs at the ball. Alongside the photo in small but important-looking lettering was *David Nunley/Pacific Image.* He bought five copies and made a spectacle of himself squeezing into a crowded elevator just as the doors were closing.

His co-workers seemed impressed and patted him on the back, though Vince seemed peeved that David had left work. In a sudden sweat and after a funny look from Gene, David wondered if he'd compromised himself by showing a photo of people in flaming drag. But he carried on, acting as though it was nothing extraordinary.

Vince tried to imagine how David would look dressed up.

That evening one of the TVs in the photo called to say that if his wife or one of her friends recognized him from the picture his marriage would be over.

In the flush of his small success David temporarily put aside memories of his evening with Pat. He knew that if he tried he could probably locate her through some of the Society members from Palo Alto. But she had his phone number and knew where he lived — after all, she had dropped him off. *If there's anything between us she'll get in touch.* Besides, he'd been busy in the darkroom.

David happened to be walking downtown on Market Street during his noon hour one day when his roving eye detected something interesting in the weave of moving bodies — a woman crossing the street toward him. A quick glance revealed that the woman was one of the transvestites from the Society probably trying to live as a woman. She was in her late forties, dressed conservatively. Obviously, David thought, she had studied the kind of woman she wanted to be and had imitated her down to the last detail. The woman had seemed oblivious to him, not even casting a glance in his direction.

David wondered if he would ever try a daylight foray and how much of a thrill it would be. Then he thought about Karen, who called herself Karen Various — that sense of humor of hers — and the hormones she was taking.

Jeanette and David had recently thrown a little party for some friends, including Karen and Jean. Karen had come alone dressed as a man. But he had worn a semi-transparent shirt and everyone could see budding breasts and darkening, expanding nipples underneath. Jeanette had been mildly upset and no one had been comfortable enough to talk about the sensation. David too had been ill at ease. He liked things to be less ambiguous — either you look like a man or a woman.

Along the same lines, some new types were showing up at The Parlour get-togethers. They called themselves gender-fuckers and came in dresses along with mustaches. One came in a sequined dress with a flat chest and hairy legs ending in tennis shoes. These newcomers brewed controversy among the regulars. Should these clowns be asked to leave or could they be the wave of the future? After all, some of the original members had been pretty far out in their own time.

David had gotten into a habit which was with him everywhere. He liked to imagine how a given man might look if dressed as a woman. David was positive that given the right wig, makeup and clothing, a good number of men could pass quite successfully as beautiful women. Conversely, he looked at women, especially on the bus, and imagined them dressed as men, with men's haircuts. He thought that the main non-reproductive difference between the sexes was the way they adorned themselves.

Mother,

I guess I'd like to brag a bit about some things that have happened to me recently.

Number one is that I've been selling some of my photos through a stock photo agency.

Number two, and not the least, is that one of my photos is in the current issue of TIME magazine in the section about "Leisure-Time America." I finally feel like I'm getting somewhere with my photography.

David

They called on Sunday when rates were low. A faraway-sounding woman's voice asked, "David?"

"David, this is mother."

"Well, hello!" His enthusiasm was hollow and he had the distinct impression of being visited in prison.

"David, your father and I are so proud of you. We went out after we got your letter and bought the copy of TIME and saw your photograph in it. We're so happy for you."

"Thank you. It was a surprise. I couldn't believe it when I saw it."

There was a short silence. "We never thought anyone in our family would be published in a national magazine."

"This is just a one-time thing, though."

"Here's Dad."

David gulped and felt something stick in his throat. He coughed and wasn't sure he could speak.

"David, it's really something to be published in a magazine like TIME. Your picture looked very professional."

"Though the subjects were off-color."

"You know, you've reached the top when you get in a magazine the caliber of TIME."

They were all too nice to each other, but the subject of David's dressing was never discussed. After the call David leaned back in his chair and balanced on its rear legs by touching the wall behind him. So his parents had taken the big first step. But they'd never be comfortable with his transvestitism. They probably thought it was something he could excise like a mole or corn. It seemed they were better off pretending that the TV side of him didn't exist.

On the other hand, he felt like he was a little boy again in the sunny back yard of his childhood with his parents stroking his head and saying, "You're such a good little boy." It seemed that a compromise was in the works. He'd be good and they'd forget his transgressions. He tried to balance on the two legs of his chair without touching the wall and was able to hang in suspended animation for as long as ten seconds.

That evening David dreamed many dreams and recorded several in his diary. In one, he was visiting a house occupied only by women. In one of the women's rooms he looked through drawers and found a filmy blue bra, which he fondled. The woman it belonged to came in and saw it and his erection. She took this as something usual and went about her business. He knew then that the women accepted him and that touching the bra was just part of the total sensuousness of the world.

In the other dream he was riding on a bus with some eager Japanese touring San Francisco. The bus driver, David's father as a younger man, was explaining the history of the city over a PA system. While the tourists were all on one side of the bus photographing buffalo in Golden Gate Park, David idly looked out the other side and saw a very high radio tower which resembled the Eiffel Tower. Some college students were climbing it as part of a zany fraternity stunt. Before they reached the top David found himself climbing above them. The tower was being blown in a strong wind, swaying dangerously. Eventually David was confident enough to hold on to the tower with one hand and swing out from it. He wanted his father to see him, but he was still describing the buffalo scene to the tourists.

After two weeks, he still hadn't heard from Pat and was wondering if he'd been a one-night stand.

Pat, however, had been starring in some of his masturbation fantasies. In one, he pictured her being filmed for a porno movie. She was deliciously dressing up in a man's rough clothing. He dwelt on a scene where she was pulling on long, thick socks over smooth limbs. Seeming slim and muscular, she lay down and began to massage her clit under white jockey shorts.

Then he imagined her pointing a pistol at him and forcing him to dress as a woman. Finally she ordered him to accompany her down a busy street, she wearing a man's pinstripe suit and him a loose-fitting dress. People could see that he was male and looked at him curiously. Pat walked proudly like Diana Rigg.

The Diana Society's social night at The Parlour was refreshingly like the old days—there were no gender-fuckers—except for the news that the get-togethers wouldn't be held there any more. The Society's new president didn't get along with the management.

Josie, the bus driver who always wore satin, was at the bar talking to Charlotte the warehouseman who never quite lost his burly voice. Next to him was his wife Sandra. At one of the tables was Jimmy Kim in male clothing along with Dedee Chu, who worked as a waiter in an expensive restaurant as a female. Susan, a petite commercial artist taking hormones, and Rose, a shy college student, filled out the table.

David-as-Natalie had walked from home again nearly without a second thought, past the junior high school and the archdiocese offices, past the ice cream shop and the blue collar restaurant. At one point she began to whistle a tune, not sure where she'd heard it before.

Finally she waved to the Gypsy fortuneteller in her storefront and made her way across the busy traffic of Market Street. The fabric of her dress swirled around her as she walked. Men were looking.

Call me dangerous.

In the cozy bar Natalie was pleasantly surprised. Her photos of the ball had been published in the Society's newsletter and there were orders for extra prints. A glass of wine made her feel even better. Soon Karen came in looking impish and sat down for some girl talk. Yes, her breasts were still growing. No, her patients didn't seem to notice—or didn't *want* to notice. Jean was getting turned off by the changes. That didn't seem to bother Karen terribly—she was concentrating on forming the wardrobe she'd wear as a real woman. On the recommendation of her shrink, Karen had decided to live as a woman full time before she was sex-changed.

Natalie grew disturbed as she listened to Karen chatting on like a songbird, sometimes creating elaborate fantasies about her upcoming womanhood. Natalie wondered just how stringent the screening process was for sex-change operations and how much counseling pre-operative patients got. There had always been something whimsical and screwy about Karen and now that part of her seemed to be taking over. And she was a doctor for Christ's sake.

The new president of the Society, a big-shouldered broad, came by to ask if either of them knew of another bar where the socials could be held. Was there another simpatico gay bar? Natalie, irritated at her for losing The Parlour, so close to home, was about to answer when she felt cool and gentle hands cover her eyes.

She impulsively slipped her head around, twisting her wig slightly. There stood Pat, resplendent in a tweed sports coat and black turtleneck sweater, with a warm smile.

"I can't believe it! You beautiful woman! How'd you know I'd be here?"

"Jeanette told me when I dropped by the house."

Natalie absorbed some of the warmth emanating from the figure standing before her, combined with a dusky fragrance that might have been perfume.

Natalie introduced Karen. "Won't you join us? Would you like some wine?"

"Gee, I'm sorry but my daughter is out in the car. Why don't you come out and meet her? I can't bring her in here."

Natalie was less than excited.

Danielle Wending was two and a half years old, a quiet blonde. She looked at the stranger seated next to her in their Volvo station wagon only when she could hold on to her mother. Pat gave her to Natalie, who felt ridiculous holding her. She'd left the easygoing part of herself back in the bar. Now she was a guy wearing greasy makeup and a wig.

"Hello, Danielle," he said, lowering his artificial voice a notch. He asked Pat if her daughter had met TVs before.

Pat nodded yes. But the little one pouted and put her hands to her eyes as if to cry. David tried to pull her closer to his bosom and then she actually did cry.

"Well, I tried."

"She doesn't know you. Don't feel bad. I just wanted you to meet her." Danielle immediately stopped crying as Pat took her back, then the toddler looked intently at David again.

"She's a very cute girl," he allowed.

After a pleasant bite to eat in The Parlour's restaurant, an invitation to Pat's home was extended and quickly accepted. On the freeway in San Francisco, with Danielle asleep in her car seat in the back, Pat drove by the giant bubbling glass of beer atop Hamm's brewery. They had stopped to pick up some male clothes at his flat, but he remained dressed as a woman.

"Love your outfit," he said as they passed gentle hills lit with the scattered embers of distant street lights.

"It's my favorite. I wore it because I hoped I'd find you tonight."

"I feel so lucky to see you again." He paused. "I'm just a little curious. Why didn't you get in touch before? I was beginning to think I was a one-nighter. *I* have an excuse—I forgot to get your phone number and address."

Pat was driving at ten over the limit. "Well, it wasn't because I didn't want to see you, believe me."

David waited.

"I suppose I'd better tell you. I have a friend, a guy from out East. He's a research biologist, a well-known one—Marty's his name—and guess what, he's a TV. He was just out visiting. He's quite taken with me and tends to be very jealous. So I didn't want you calling or anything."

"How do you feel about him?"

They both looked back to see Danielle asleep, clutching a doll.

"Friends." She smiled. "I think he's a brilliant guy and all. He's really into dressing. The guy flies all the way out here from the East Coast to be with me and dress maybe three times a year. But whether he realizes it or not he's too involved with his research to have a relationship. He calls a lot. Very intense person. Very funny sometimes, too."

"How does he look dressed?"

"Pretty nice. He can afford the best. He knows his makeup. Last time he actually flew out in drag."

"You seem to have an affinity for transvestites."

"I do. You're probably thinking I'm some sort of TV den mother."

They both laughed.

David grew silent again and looked out at the night. Stars were showing above the nearly deserted freeway that lazily followed the contours of wooded hills. Pat's features were softly defined by the warm glow from the instrument panel, yet she still had the look of a determined woman.

He had begun to whistle under his breath before he became consciously aware of it. Again, he wondered what the tune was—

it was the same one he'd whistled on the street earlier. It was so
familiar—

"I feel comfortable with TVs," she was saying. "After all, in
my own way I'm kind of one myself."

"That part of you turns me on in more ways than you could
imagine."

"When I'm dressing in guy clothes I feel more together. I just
like heftier clothes. Sometimes I'll dress frilly like a woman, but
just as something different to do, not the way I like to be most of
the time."

"You were a tomboy, I suppose."

"I grew up on a sheep ranch my dad owned in Wyoming. I
don't think I wore a dress once until I was in high school." She
explained that both of her parents were dead, her father in a truck
accident, then her mother of a heart attack several years later.
And Pat, the only child, had come into a modest inheritance.

Pat exited the 280 freeway and slowly angled down into the
quiet streets of Palo Alto. As she entered a cul-de-sac, David
made out *Marwood Court* on a street sign. As they pulled into the
driveway of a darkened, pleasant-looking small house he was
suddenly uneasy. *This is where I want to be, isn't it?*

Danielle was put to bed after being carried in over Pat's
shoulder. Then in her softly-lit living room Pat and David sat on a
sofa and looked into each other's eyes. Pat reached out and
touched his face. They kissed gently.

After getting up and pouring him wine, Pat went to a closet,
found a gift-wrapped package and smilingly handed it to him.
Never a great present-giver himself, he was always taken aback
and pleasured when someone gave him one.

"This *is* a surprise."

"Just open it, kid."

Inside the wrapping was a slim box with a Fredericks of
Hollywood logo.

"What a wet dream!" He was looking at a red satin corset,
the most erotic he'd ever touched. The cups had just the right
amount of tasteful decoration and stiffness. Its sides were lightly
boned and there were dainty garter straps.

"Aren't you going to put it on? You should know that it
wasn't easy to find. I had to go to the San Jose store to find a tall
one."

When he came out of the bathroom he felt like the lead in the *Rocky Horror Show*. Pat, meanwhile, had changed into soft corduroy trousers and a starched white shirt under a soft sweater. Her hair was pulled back again masculinely.

"It's just a little small," she said as she had him turn around. "How does it feel?"

"It's so nice and tight." For a moment, David compared this scene to his scenes with Diane.

At that moment his penis chose to spring loose from under the corset and hung in the air. Pat put her hand around it as David quivered and stood for a moment on his toes.

"All right, big boy," she said as though talking to his member, "get your dress back on and we'll take care of you." She grabbed his ass and squeezed it hard.

In bed the next morning after a tumultuous coming together, Pat wanted to know about David's growing up as a TV. David was back in a male mode.

"I don't know for sure why I got into it. For a long time I read every psychology and psychoanalytic book I could but they didn't tell me much.

"My dressing has always been pretty sexual. But when I was a kid sex was never discussed—it was all a mystery. I started by getting off on lingerie ads. The bras seemed so perfect, you know, like they were on Greek goddesses or something. Then I started wearing my mother's lingerie and stuff when I was alone. I even stole some of her things."

"Didn't she ever find out?"

"I was so careful she never knew anything. Or if she did she never let on. Finally when I came out here to California I could do whatever I wanted and began to get serious about the whole thing."

"You're from Ohio, right? That's where your parents live now?"

"*Newsome*, Ohio. Yeah, they're still there. Listen, I've got to tell you how it was growing up there. Can I bore you?"

"Yes, please bore me."

"I can remember wearing my mother's clothes while everyone from my family was away at church. I'd hear the church bells ring and know that other boys my age were walking to church like little saints while I was sinning my ass off. I'd beat off and then try to destroy every last shred of evidence of what I was doing."

Pat tried to suppress a laugh. "No, I'm not laughing at you. I just remembered this thing that happened in high school. I had a big crush on one of the football players, and he didn't even know I existed. They called him Truck. Truxtin was his real name. He had the neatest snakeskin cowboy boots. One time I appropriated them and took 'em home. You know how pointy cowboy boots are. You know how one might kinda fit in down here—" She pointed between her legs. "They provided some great solitary sex."

They traded stories, luxuriating in a Saturday morning bed. Danielle came trotting in later to crawl in bed with them. Pat had explained the night before that Dannie was from her seven-year marriage to the part owner of a small electronics parts company. Bought out by his partners, he'd grown distant and hostile even though he too was a TV. "Believe it or not I didn't know what a transvestite was before we got married." He'd spent too much of his time tooling around at night on his motorcycle. Since the breakup Patricia had been supporting her abbreviated family by running a computerized rental-finder service.

When David returned to the city that afternoon he was giddy, his brain occupied with the memory of Pat's body against his. It occurred to him that she combined the best of both worlds. She had a strong, mother-like, nurturing quality besides being a temptress.

As days went by things seemed different. The world was happier. He noticed that when he walked the few blocks from the bus to work he was more aware of smiles than frowns. Pleasurable ideas were bounding around and expanding inside him. The glow and excitement was also mildly threatening. If he didn't watch himself be could become silly. He'd been that way briefly with Corky and Diane, too, but without any trust.

One day out walking during the noonhour he found himself whistling that familiar tune again. Then while he was listening to an offbeat FM station that evening he heard it once more—and it finally registered as the tune his father used to whistle when he was preoccupied.

At work David plodded on, struggling to stay awake, watching the clock, imagining he was slipping down a hillside of scattered, slippery file folders. He continued to rue the fact that he wasn't making enough at photography to quit. He and Gene weren't talking. Vince Grasso was his usual white-bread self.

On another front, David slacked off production of stock photos for Sam and Pacific Images and spent most of his time producing the desert prints. In the late hours of the night he hung out in his red-lit darkroom, and amid the smells of sulfur and acetic acid relived his Anza-Borrego trip. This was the nitty gritty of it all—developing pieces of silvered paper that sometimes responded magically and sometimes cursed him. But the more time he devoted to the darkroom the better a printmaker he became.

Midway through the process of making his large prints he brought some samples to a professional studio photographer he'd once been introduced to. The feisty old man, who'd become somewhat shaky in his later years and whose assistants did much of his work, gave him fifteen minutes. Mr. Stanton's close-cropped hair and neatly-trimmed beard were white, and David watched as the man lit his pipe and put on bifocals that hung from a chain around his neck.

"It's just my opinion, of course," he said, "but your prints overall need more contrast. Also, I think a warmer paper would fit your subjects better. Your blacks should be blacker. Do you use toner?"

David shook his head no, and wrote down Stanton's recommendations.

The old man complimented David on his shooting and conception, however. When David explained that he was trying for a show, Stanton phoned a friend who ran the municipal gallery downtown. "George," he said, "I've got a young man here who should get a show at your place."

Evidently the elder photographer's recommendation carried some weight because David was given an appointment to see the curator. As he was leaving, David was told by one of Stanton's assistants that "I've only seen the old man do this for one other person," and he named a well-known nature photographer.

David returned to his darkroom with a head of steam that carried him past 20 new prints in two weeks. He spotted, mounted and wrapped them and took the stack in a handsome new carrying case to George at the Irons Gallery. George noncommittally looked at the prints while talking about everything but. Finally David was forced to ask him point-blank if he was going to get a show.

"Oh, yes, yes. Didn't I tell you? Didn't I make it clear? Oh, yes, Mr. Nunley. Anyone that Mr. Stanton recommends is quite fine with us. Don't mind me. It's just that I enjoy talking so much to artists. I'm sorry if we had a misunderstanding, I really am." And so on.

David left with directions on how to prepare his work for the exhibition and a firm date for it in April. When he told Jeanette—"My first show!"—she said he deserved it and shook his hand like an old-fashioned pump handle. David insisted on a bear hug. Jeanette promised to cater the event, five months away.

17

David began to invent reasons why Pat would leave him. He wrote them in his diary, not so much that he believed them, but to expose them to the light of day.

He wrote that she'd tire of him because he was dull, or because he wouldn't get along with Danielle. Then there was the fact that he lived too far away. She'd find someone closer and more exciting, someone who was more loving.

Several times when Pat phoned, David felt sluggish and unresponsive. Finally she asked why. He said he didn't know. "Probably something passing," he said. She asked if she'd done something wrong. "No, no, it's nothing like that," he said.

One quiet weekend at 36 Marwood Court, David dragged around the house. He was making an extra effort to be friendly with Danielle, helping her feed her pet rabbits. When Dannie went to bed in the evening Pat helped David become Natalie. Then they went to cuddle on the sofa and watch Masterpiece Theater. David was silent and stiff.

"David, what is it?"

"I don't know. I really don't know. I feel out of it."

"I don't think you want to be here."

"But I do," he protested, wondering what miscalculation had gotten him in this jam. After a long, heavy silence he said meekly, "I wish you'd tie me up and whip me."

"So that's what you've been thinking about all this time." She sat back and looked up at the ceiling like an awkwardly-propositioned college student. "I don't like to see you like this. Why do you want to be punished? You remind me of some religious flagellant."

"It's exciting. I fantasize about it. Haven't you ever been turned on by pain?"

"Oh yeah, biting and so on. But I draw the line when the whips and chains come in. I'm not a hardware person." She chuckled.

He was at least relieved to air his secrets. He realized that she'd behaved exactly as he'd wanted her to. He worried, though, that he'd made himself too weak before her and that she might want to push him away as Corky and Diane had done.

He changed his position on the sofa. "Let's do something different."

"Like?"

"I know this sounds crazy, but let's camp out, outside the house, like we used to do when we were kids."

"We can't leave Danielle alone in here. But hey, we could get out the sleeping bags and sleep right here on the living room rug. We'll just open the patio doors all the way and it'll be like being outside."

They zipped two bags together. Then, makeup and female accouterments removed, David enjoyed cuddling for a time. He felt the heat of her body, the heat that both comforted and burned. Eventually they turned their backs to each other and dozed off. Sometime during the night David heard rain spattering on the bricks and plants in the patio. A cool, wet air slid over his cheeks and into his nostrils. He relaxed, imagining himself to be in a tent in a deep redwood forest, protected from the elements. He turned over on his side and Pat said something like "How'r'ya doin'?"

"It started raining. I love rain."

"That's nice." She immediately fell back asleep. David lay a few minutes longer, feeling microdrops of rain hit his face. Then he too went back to sleep.

He worried about his moodiness, and thought he shouldn't overdo being with Pat. So he told her on the phone that the following weekend he was going hiking in the woods "to be by myself a little and take some pictures." Instead, he wound up staying at home, lazing around the house and taking in a movie. Sunday morning he answered the phone. It was Pat.

"I thought you were going out hiking."

"Changed my mind. Didn't feel up to it."

"Something funny's going on with you."

"Oh, hell," said David, getting an instant headache, "I'm getting in over my head. Things are getting too complicated."

"Well, I certainly don't want to give you any complications," she said, and hung up.

David thought about dressing up to help his mood, but it didn't seem to fit. No doubt about it, he was involved with this woman. Maybe he did love her. The only problem now was that she wouldn't be mean to him—she wouldn't whip or reject him. *Now I'm forcing her to do that too, in my own way.*

He finally walked over to Castro Street and ate in an expensive gay restaurant where the waiter was much too formal. The VA clerk doodled on a napkin gloomily, sure he was the only single person in the restaurant. He replayed his relationship once more. Surely he'd taken Pat too much for granted. She'd been an absolute angel, so supportive of him and his crossdressing.

He remembered her coming for him at The Parlour and how he'd thought only of his own embarrassment when he'd first met Danielle. What had he done for the two of them, anyway? The surprise was that the relationship had gone as far as it did. Maybe it was because he was a good fuck. *Yeah, sure.* David suspected that Pat was this nice to whomever she became involved with.

The cold winter winds of November were blowing, drying out streets wet from an earlier storm. On his evening walk home from yet another restaurant—eating out improved his morale—

he kept himself warm inside a down jacket. Alone again. Who would he spend Christmas with? He'd alienated Pat, and Jeanette planned to go visit relatives in Sonoma. He would end up all alone. In the old days when he was in college in Michigan he could still return home to spend the holidays with his parents.

But he was a big boy now. Maybe he could go down and take pictures at one of the charity dining rooms that gave free meals on Christmas Day. He could get in line himself in old clothing to get an idea of how it was at the bottom of the heap.

He thought about his upcoming show. *Pictures of the desert,* he muttered to himself. *Some kind of phony mysticism. Something in vogue now. I should really be out photographing people like bums and prostitutes and workers.* He kicked himself for channeling his energies into safe, uncontroversial photography.

Upon returning home, he got into a discussion about Pat with Jeanette. Uncharacteristically, he asked her for advice.

"Do you love her?" Jeanette asked abruptly. They sat at the wooden table where they always talked, the table where they did the monthly bills.

"I honestly don't know what the word means. What do you mean by love?"

"You're kidding."

"I mean, it's misused. Everybody says love, love, love, like it's water out of the tap."

"Well then. Do you like to be with her a lot? Do you think about her a lot?"

He took his time before answering. "I feel like I want to be with her some of the time. I certainly think about her a lot but I don't want to be taken over by her."

"Does she love you?"

"I think so. She said so a couple times, but I'm not sure if she really means it. I'll tell you this, though—I think she likes me quite a bit more than I like her. That's the kind of person she is. She's more generous and loving—there's that word—than I am. That's one of the things that bothers me. I know I can't give back equal amounts."

David began to wonder if he should be so candid with a woman whose own choice of partners left something to be desired.

Jeanette looked serious. "I'll tell you something. I like Pat and I think you're alike in many ways."

David urged her on.

"You both are honorable people."

"Honorable. God, what an unusual word to use. About the last one I'd expect."

"And you both seem to be into magic. I mean, I can see this by your both dressing up to change yourselves."

"Magic. That's a nice way to look at it. But you know that Pat's daughter complicates things."

"Sometime you're going to have to come to terms with kids. When you accept yourself then you can accept kids."

David laughed. "Jeanette, you're a goddamn oracle. I've never seen this in you before, but I should have known."

David stopped going to society meetings. The club had gone further in its decline and now seemed to exist chiefly as a newsletter and a few scattered meetings in homes. There was, however, a very active chapter in Pensacola, Florida. David put on panties once in awhile or wore a bra in the stressful environment of the darkroom where he constantly had to make decisions. He wrote several letters to Pat but pitched them all in the wastepaper when he thought he was chicken not to call—and he didn't call because he felt weak.

At nine o'clock one evening something clicked and he phoned her, "just to say hello."

"Well, hello."

"I've missed you."

"I was wondering." Silence.

"Ah . . . What I need to say . . ." —the words wanted to come out like blood from a cut artery— "is that I'd really like to be with you and Danielle for Christmas if t-that would be possible."

"We'd love to have you. But there's one thing. Marty asked to come out for Christmas and I said yes."

David remembered her descriptions of the research biologist.

"Oh. Then you wouldn't want me to come."

"You're so silly. You can both be here as far as I'm concerned, if you don't mind being around him."

"I guess not. I'd like to meet him." David's throat clenched.

At work the women put together a Christmas office party and the head of the local VA district came by on his annual visit to tell them what good team players they were.

David inwardly smirked. If he, David, were the big boss he would sure as hell visit installations more than once a year. Sitting on a desk across the way was Gene Gatzo, laughing at the director's heavy-handed jokes. The grapevine had it that Gene had been seeing a new woman for several months. David had finally seen her pick Gene up one day after work—a slender woman with so-so hair. On the other hand, she'd been driving a new Audi so maybe she did have something on the ball.

As the party drew to a close, David and Gene had a few tentative words. Across the way, even though only non-alcoholic punch had been served, The Jock had managed to become inebriated. Mrs. Johnson took Polaroid pictures, David wore red-lace panties under his clothes and Vince Grasso loosened up to sponsor a few toasts.

David felt a jerk as a Southern Pacific engine pulled his passenger car out of San Francisco's train station on Christmas Day. Children traveling to holiday gatherings watched out the windows as the many pairs of tracks gradually narrowed to two. David hoped the gray skies overhead would clear. After all, what was Christmas without some sun?

He liked riding trains, especially since they went by people's back yards, through long tunnels and behind the facades of well-known businesses, which often turned out to be junky and overgrown with weeds.

In a few minutes he'd meet Pat and Marty. He had Marty pegged as a kind of Carl Sagan in heels, an intense, friendly guy. David expected he'd have to play second fiddle to the intruder. He checked to make sure he still had his travel bag next to him. Within it were Christmas gifts and his ammunition—a favorite dress, makeup, and lingerie.

Ten minutes after he called from the Palo Alto train station the familiar shape of Pat's station wagon rounded a far corner. His heart raced. It had been a long time. She unlocked the door and he got in. She had dressed carelessly, making her look over-weight.

"It's so good to see you," said David, giving her a perfunctory kiss. "Are you mad at me?"

"Of course not," said Pat, allowing a wan smile to creep across her tight lips.

"I almost forgot to say Merry Christmas—"

"Yes, well, it certainly is Christmas, no doubt about that."

As she drove away, he decided to lay low. He wondered if he'd feel like dressing if she was acting this way. Suddenly he didn't like the drift of things.

"Pat, I don't think it's going to work today," he said in a small voice. "I think you'd better just leave me on the corner here. I'll catch a train back." There were tears in his eyes.

Pat pulled to one side of the street abruptly and said, "You think I'm mad at you. Well, I'll tell you. It's Marty. He's been here two days now, all the time in drag. First off, when he heard about our relationship and that you were coming, he behaved like a jealous child. Then he wanted to marry me—right away. He's been like glue—he just attaches himself to me. I'm afraid he's a little off his rocker." She let loose a pent-up breath and looked at David with tired eyes.

"Oh." David imagined a harried female pigeon being chased by a single-minded cock pigeon.

"So, my friend, that's what you're walking into on Christmas Day. Marty's back there now, cooking things for dinner. I'm trying to keep him occupied."

Marty was a model of politeness when David arrived. She wore a curly blonde wig, pants and blouse. There was a resemblance to a middle-class English woman on a holiday.

Marty was behaving so like a woman, busily measuring flour and spices for a pumpkin bread, that her feminine presence seemed quite natural. David wondered how long the Easterner could maintain her frenetic pace. *Busy, busy.* David announced that he'd dress up later, giving him some time to play a new board game with Danielle, who'd received it from her absent father.

When David did finally dress, the taut magic of attiring himself for his eyes only was missing. The only spark of enjoyment came when he put on makeup, which transformed his face enjoyably. At two in the afternoon, with sunlight breaking through the overcast and pouring in through patio windows, they all sat down to the Great American Spread. The ritual of eating always put David-as-Natalie in a better mood.

"You two worked so hard on this," Natalie said, sitting erect and proper, "that I hereby promise to do all the cleanup."

"Hear, hear," said Pat, smiling. "You've got yourself a deal." She had transformed herself, now wearing an Asian-print dress with a low V-neckline. A black velvet choker and silver earrings contrasted nicely with her lightly-powdered face. Her hair gorgeously cascaded down from a barrette.

Danielle played with her potatoes and gravy. "Have some turkey, Dannie," her mother coaxed.

"I think she saw me make my potatoes this way," said Natalie, pointing to the gravy lake she'd carved in the middle of her mashed potatoes.

"Davie dress like you, mommy. Davie look like you."

Natalie didn't think she'd embarrass that easily, but she did. Why didn't she say that about Marty?

"Davie likes to dress that way sometimes. But now you should call him Natalie, because that's his girl name."

"Dannie like to dress that way now." All those around the table laughed.

"You can dress up, sure you can," said Pat, "but let's eat first."

Natalie's long, hippie-girl wig put her in a softer, more feminine mood, and she felt more comfortable with Marty. She asked the guest about her trip west.

"They almost got me," Marty said speedily, looking at Pat, who'd obviously heard the story.

She explained that she'd stopped midway in St. Louis to see some relatives. On the way to a motel in a rented car—she was in drag—a cop stopped her for a bad brake light.

"He asked for my ID. I showed him my male driver's license. He kept popping questions—what was I doing here, and so on. Finally I just showed him my card from the Sexual Identity Forum which explains why I dress. Then he backed off, but he said I should be careful. Phewww! So I came the rest of the way here as a male."

"You're brave," said Natalie.

"Brave or stupid."

Natalie began to appreciate Marty's plucky spirit and energy, as though the woman's mainspring had many more years before it would wind down. Natalie herself was already tiring from food and wine but managed to get Marty to talk about her high-tech job and failed marriage.

Patricia Wending lay in her darkened bedroom with a faint patch of moonlight falling across a curious scene. On one side, Marty's coifed head lay over Pat's arm. A couple tears ran down her cheeks, eroding her makeup. Pat couldn't see them, but felt them on her arm. On the other side Natalie lay stiffly, similarly held.

Marty whispered, "I am so turned on by you."

"I know."

"And I can't do anything about it."

Natalie had slipped into a favorite nightgown. She moved her hand to cup Pat's breast. That way they all fell asleep.

The next morning Natalie-as-David got up early to leave for work. Making toast and cutting up a banana over cereal, he startled when something touched his back. It was Danielle. David was hungry to respond to her freshness. She was after some breakfast too and wanted what he was having. He felt on an even plane with her for once in this little oasis of time.

"Can tie shoe?" she asked, holding her tiny sneakers.

Danielle's mother eventually ventured out in her bathrobe, looking rather down-to-earth again, saying that Marty was still sleeping after a restless night. Pat was in a buoyant mood and had breakfast with them.

When he left for work it was with a warmth, a feeling that domestic tranquillity might just be possible. As he lightly napped on the train back to San Francisco, though, someone threw a rock against his window. After the shock of that, he settled back and replayed the events at Pat's. A resentment against Marty set in. *I'll bet he'll whine until Pat gives him her body. I'm glad he's leaving. I hope he doesn't come back.*

18

When David went on to work on the bus that same day, the downtown seemed to have fewer people than usual. Arriving at the VA building, he was chagrined to learn from the guard that it was a federal holiday and he had the day off. In the old days David would've read about it in the newspaper, but lately there had been distractions. He returned home to an empty flat because Jeanette hadn't returned from her holiday trip. He was at loose ends. After napping fitfully for an hour in his chilly bedroom, feeling a phantom Pat next to him, he responded to an elemental need to get outside. Boarding an ancient 'L' trolley car on 17th Street, he headed for the ocean with his camera.

As he sat in his customary slumped position in the car he returned to thoughts of Danielle and her mother. It was odd, he thought, that he had been closest to them when another man was in the house—a competitor.

Riding the 'L' to the end of the line near the zoo, he made his way through a pedestrian tunnel to the beach. He could always count on the smell of the ocean, the cool breeze and the sound of waves to invigorate him. He left miles of footprints from one end of Ocean Beach to the other, sometimes jogging and sometimes stopping to take telephoto pictures of beach people in the hazy distance.

Then he left the beach and walked through the upper-class Seacliff district before returning to the beach at the base of the Golden Gate Bridge. The giant structure arched above him in waves of latticed steel as he heard the faint whoosh of unseen cars.

David looked out toward the ocean. Although the cold wind coming in through the Golden Gate nipped his cheeks and ears, he felt warm and secure in his thick jacket. His day had started with fears of boredom or depression but had ended up invigorating him. No wasted time, very little loneliness.

His mind began to put together the events of his recent past. Maybe he hadn't been traveling so aimlessly in his life — maybe he hadn't been squandering his time. Maybe, as on this hike, he had been on a straight, nearly pre-determined course all along. Maybe Corky, Diane and even Gene Gatzo had served a purpose.

It was curious, he thought, that when he was in a good mood, things came together. Things made sense and the world was all right again.

David made his way up past shrubs to the bridge toll area to wait for a bus. He glanced to the south and saw the new television tower being built on Twin Peaks. The last rosy rays of the setting sun were still illuminating the tall, simple structure. It stood bravely and stalwartly like a strong mother.

Halfway home on the bus he realized he was in Karen's neighborhood, got off, and walked the four blocks to her apartment. Karen answered the door and invited him in.

"This is a surprise, Natalie!" she said, looking thin in her bathrobe. The doctor's real, long hair was uncombed.

David explained where he'd been. "I feel so goddamn healthy. I should get out more often! How have you been?"

"I haven't been so fantastic. Jean left, you know. I guess you and I haven't talked for a while. Listen, I'm taking a long vacation from work while I change over to being Karen all the time. I've got the date for my operation and I can't wait! Want to see my tities?" Karen opened her bathrobe to display two small, dark-nippled breasts. Something about them seemed unnatural and faintly evil to David.

"How are you making a living?"

"No problem. There's the money I saved up and I'm helping another doctor put a medical book together. There's some editing and proofreading work."

"You seem kind of thin and cooped up here. Are you OK? How do you feel with the hormones?"

"I haven't been eating as well as I should. Not having Jean here leaves a gap. To tell the truth, nothing's going to be quite right until I have the operation. I just need to be a certified, card-carrying woman."

For a moment Karen seemed her old self. "You can see how I'm marking the days off the calendar."

Karen went to get some beers. They drank in silence. Then Karen asked if he'd like to dress up and keep her company.

"Oh, it's way too late to get into that now," said David.

"Then why don't you stay with me overnight? You could sleep on the couch or whatever."

An hour later David was trying on some of Karen's things — a bra, a dress, a beautiful wig and heels that were too small.

"Oh God, I need a shave," he said. Just then, he remembered starting the day at Patricia and Danielle's. That seemed like a week ago. Now it was nighttime and he was sinning. He fell asleep on Karen's bed dressed, with wig still on and Karen's arm around his shoulder. An hour later he woke and took off all the women's things. He slept the remainder of the night with his butt touching Karen's.

In the morning when he was pretending to sleep, Karen ever so gently began caressing his back and chest. He lay still and didn't discourage her. Karen leaned over to see if he had an erection. He did, and lay on his back to display it to the coyly smiling doctor. When Karen took its tip between two fingers, though, David could only break up in giggles. Karen tried suddenly to kiss him but David evaded like a little boy. He finally pulled Karen to him and they hugged for a long time until the alarm buzzed for David to go to work.

David ran the taste of Karen through his mind as he rode the bus downtown. Part of him took pride in being liberated, but he wouldn't return for that sort of thing. It was OK one time. If he kept doing intimate things with her, with her still-present cock and male aura, he knew he'd feel lousy.

He wondered how much of a letdown Karen would have after the operation. He pictured her in a bathrobe in the morning making coffee, then working extra hard with her makeup to try to erase all vestiges of her former masculinity. In real life, she'd find herself competing with the genuine article. *At least she's a doctor. She'll find a way to make it financially.*

He resolved not to see her again until after the operation. Then, who knows? He might even be a little jealous.

He lay in bed the next morning, a Saturday, thinking. Jeanette hadn't returned from Sonoma yet and the house was totally quiet. It would be a slow, carefree day. After Karen, the prospect of seeing Pat and Danielle again seemed positively error-free. They would all get together and behave like a family, or something like that. Everything would be clear and reasonable and filled with light and understanding. Their instincts would lead them to do the right things.

At eleven o'clock David got off the train in Palo Alto and saw Pat's Volvo waiting under the shade of a large tree. Only momentarily miffed that she hadn't gotten out to meet him, he snuck around to the back of the car. She seemed oblivious to the world, intently reading a paperback and listening to classical music. He edged around the side, hoping that no one would think him too strange. He smiled at a passer-by to allay any suspicion. Then he raised his head so he could see over her door.

He received such great enjoyment from looking at her sweet face unawares. A face in repose—calm, self-possessed, and more serious than when she knew people were looking. He wished he could photograph her that way, slouched down in the car seat, totally absorbed. In that state she could be a man, she could be a woman—but most of all she was an alive, quirky human being.

"Hi," he said softly.

Pat jumped. "The train . . . I was so involved with this book."

"I've been sitting here looking at you for the last few minutes."

"You're kidding."

Pat was, David noticed, made shy by his voyeurism. He got in the car and they kissed.

"What did you see?" she asked.

"I saw a woman in a classical painting. Maybe an Eakins. Or I can think of dozens of paintings of the Madonna."

"It must be the motherly qualities you see in me."

"I wonder if you realize how really beautiful you are."

"Like the last time I picked you up?"

"That one doesn't count."

"Well, anyway, I appreciate your telling me these things, even if they're not true. I need a hug. Give me a nice big hug."

David did just that. Hugging was like eating, drinking and breathing for Patricia. Quite necessary.

David took to spending weekends in Palo Alto. Danielle still looked at him askance sometimes but David wasn't so uncertain about her any more. If she took a temporary dislike to him, that was OK. If she took a shine to him, he didn't fall over in amazement either. He began to see her as something other than a clone of her mother.

One Saturday afternoon when Pat and Dannie were out shopping and David was alone in her house he began to look through Pat's drawers. He hated and loved sneaking around behind her back, just when they'd concluded a pact to be completely honest with each other. He found some new and previously unknown lingerie and tried it on, masturbating gloriously. He'd been missing those masturbations. That evening when they were about to go to bed—and what a soft, fluffy bed she had—she found a pair of patterned panty hose that he'd forgotten to put away. When she saw the wicked run he'd left she knew what had happened.

It wasn't so much that he'd been wearing her things as his secrecy.

"I don't know," he admitted. "I get this kick out of doing things on the sly. I mean, I enjoy our sex but there's still the old me in me too. If I shared all the sex in me, sex wouldn't be so exciting."

Pat was hard pressed to understand. "To me, sex is in the

open between people, the more in the open the better. Why should you want to hide things from me?"

And on and on it went.

"Oh Jesus," she complained. "If it's not one thing it's another."

One cold night in February when David and Jeanette were making their respective dinners in the Hancock Street apartment she offhandedly announced she was giving him 20 days' notice. She said she'd decided to go share a flat with another woman artist out in the avenues, out in the fog belt.

"You don't like it here?" he asked, taken aback.

"I've had a pretty good time."

"Then what?"

"You're going to live with Pat, aren't you?"

He smiled. "What gives you that idea?"

"You're not around here that much any more. I guess I need to have someone around more often."

"You mean you miss me? No, you wouldn't admit that."

She made one of those tilts of her head which revealed beautiful curves of cheek and lips. "Well," she said with a small smile, "one does get used to another person. We had some good talks. You were around when something needed fixing. You told the neighbors off when they made too much noise."

"I guess I wanted to hear that I was more than Mr. Fixit. But Pat and I—we haven't talked about my moving in. So your leaving kind of puts me on the spot." David thought a moment. "Maybe it's for the best. I should probably thank you."

"You're welcome," said Jeanette, scooping cooked brown rice out of an old aluminum pan.

"One thing, please. Can you still cater my photo show in April? I've been counting on you for that."

"As long as I'm still working for Virgil's."

David began to make an inspired milkshake with all kinds of exotic ingredients. He had recently bought a book titled *Better Health With Your Home Blender* from someone at work who had self-published it.

One evening Pat invited over a transvestite couple for a foursome of Scrabble. She'd met them at the Beaux Artes Ball.

The woman loved to buy her husband female things and help him cross-dress. They often went out as girlfriends—he was able to pass in public if he didn't talk. Her husband's special hobby, she was fond of saying, was no more unusual than other men's model train layouts or gun collections.

Then David and Pat visited Harvey and Margaret's—such were their names—and they had begun a routine. Harvey and David would dress fully as women while Pat would dress masculinely, with earrings. Margaret was always Margaret, with dresses.

These private get-togethers allowed David to be even more relaxed about becoming Natalie. He no longer experienced the unease he'd had when he first went out in public. What they were doing had a very middle-class taste to it. They talked about the rising crime rate, automobile gas mileages, grocery store produce departments and the best places to buy women's shoes.

Meanwhile, David was learning more about Pat's business.

She had named the business, after practical consideration, Peninsula Rental Search. Basically, she oversaw it. Five part-time employees did the front desk work and answered the phones while she, having majored in business, handled the taxes, bills, complaints, computers, payroll and advertising. Her customers were nervous, mobile techies and students from Silicon Valley looking for places to park their lives. She put in five or six hours a day in her very efficient way—sometimes taking Danielle to the office with her, sometimes to a baby-sitter. Her company's sterling reputation gave her the lion's share of the rental agency work in that part of the Bay Area.

Her part-dressing as a male enhanced her self-image as capable entrepreneur. Cowboy boots, Levi's and denim shirts were a typical work outfit.

She worried a little about David. Their emotional life had gone well enough, but she noticed his disappointment that his photography hadn't taken off. He was only earning enough at it to pay his expenses. She herself was getting on in years, thirty-six of them, and had been counting wrinkles. If she wanted any more children she'd have to commit herself now and she did want at least one more. She wished that David would consent to work in her business, but every time she'd broached it he'd backed away.

Her conservative, retired neighbors on Marwood Court knew she was different, given her penchant for male clothing, the animals in her back yard and her unmarried status. Since she'd hooked into the transvestite crowd there had been many a knotted-brow glance in her direction.

Jeanette had been out of David's apartment for a month when the time for his show arrived. He'd been spending so much time at Pat's that someone had broken into his flat and stolen some of his camera equipment and a pot plant on the back porch.

He took a day off work to hang the show and—after Pat's urging—bought a new sweater and trousers for the opening. Even though he'd mailed announcements to friends and the media, he worried that no one would come.

David and Pat—Dannie in his arms—walked into the gallery on Grove Street the evening of the opening. Jeanette and an assistant had preceded them, setting up a wonderfully inventive spread of hors d'oeuvres.

Pat wore the same outfit she had on when she picked him up at The Parlour—for luck, she said. He wore a loose, tied-at-the-waist pair of white yoga pants that, if one looked hard enough, showed the faintest outline of black underwear.

The photography critic for *ARTnews* was also there, along with Arnold Stanton, the photographer. Stanton as usual was non-committal. The kindest thing he said was that "Your prints look better. Try toning them with a stronger solution next time."

David was not to have more than five minutes with any one person for the next two hours. Several photography critics who buzzed through quickly on their rounds of galleries were polite and interested. One asked for an extra print to accompany a review. Finally, there was an inebriated young man who said the photographs were passé and proceeded to spray circles of shaving cream on the sidewalk outside. Diane made a brief appearance with her son and Laura in tow, saying, "It's not my thing but you've done a great job."

The entire context under which David had photographed the desert began to escape him. Now the photographs were all caged up and on display like animals in a zoo. David pondered all this as he sat on the commode in the men's room, shaking a little from the excitement, looking down at the little hairs on his winter-white legs and the black panties at his ankles. He had trapped the butterflies. Now all that mattered was the price.

He sold five prints outright and promised Jeanette two of her favorites.

When it was over, after countless finger foods and cheese cubes and burgundy, and after a half hour of conversation with a street philosopher who wouldn't let him out the front door, David took Pat and Danielle to Adrienne's Italian restaurant in North Beach. Amid lacy white tablecloths and romantic wine-glasses, he felt expansive and happy. The event that he had planned, worried about and worked on for so long had come to pass, and it had succeeded. The old David, the drab, underground newspaper photographer who'd been paid peanuts by the *Real Times*, was history.

He wished he was rich so he could overwhelm Pat with expensive gifts. The reality was that he was a guest in the home of an independent businesswoman. Still, he had to ask the question.

He fumbled for words and reached out to touch her hand. "I have to ask you this. I'm not the kind who can speak very well, but I would really love to be able to live with you and Danielle. You both have been really close to me, and . . . I don't like living by myself any more. Would you mind a crazy guy like me?"

A big tear slipped down Pat's cheek. "Yes. A thousand yesses. I love you, David." More tears wet her cheek. A tear escaped David's eye too and he felt himself going soft.

Danielle seemed worried. She'd seldom seen her mother cry.

"David Nunley, I know you," said Pat. "You had to have a success before you could take a step like this." She smiled the most soul-melting smile he'd ever seen and said again, "I love you so, so much." They held hands across the table and then both held Dannie's hands too. The girl smiled shyly. David for once felt thoroughly genuine, and didn't care what the waiter thought.

"Dannie have new daddy now?"

David reached over and put her on his lap. "Can I be your

new daddy? If you want me to, I'll be your daddy." The girl became very animated, reached up to touch his cheek and grinned an exuberant "Yes."

That evening in bed, Pat and David lay in each other's arms.
"Honey?"
"Yes?" David said sleepily.
"Have you ever — well, let me put it this way . . ."
"Yes?"
"I want to live with you but I need more commitment than that, too."
David was still.
"You seem to be tense," Pat said.
"I am, I suppose." He shifted to pull away from her slightly. "I know what you're going to say."
"What?"
"You think we should get married somewhere down the road."
"You said it. How do you feel about the venerable institution?"
"I suppose with a child in consideration it would be the right thing to do. I'll be honest, though. It scares me. I want to go one step at a time. I mean, just a year ago I was a dirty old man living by myself, beating off behind drawn shades. I've been on a crash course on how to live with other human beings."
"I know. I appreciate that. Let's give us a few months and then sit down and talk about it, OK?"
They were instantly asleep. It was three a.m.

Dear Mother and Dad --
   Sorry I haven't answered your last few letters. The excuse is that so many things have been happening.
   I have recently moved (I received your last letter forwarded) to 36 Marwood Court in Palo Alto, ZIP 94306, where I'm living with Patricia Wending and

her daughter from an earlier marriage, Danielle. Dannie is three years old and quite a kid.

I want you to know that this is not a fly-by-night coming together. Pat and I are quite serious about each other and who knows, there may be further developments.

Love, David and Pat

P.S. David tells me that I should write something. Just to say that you have a wonderful son who is a fine photographer and makes our house complete once again! I hope to meet you sometime soon. David has told me all about his growing up there in Ohio and it would be fun to visit sometime.

Pat

19

"That's the dress you were wearing the night we met," said Pat as David carefully hung the plastic-covered gown in her closet.

"I haven't worn it since, except once when I used it to whack off in. It's kind of a religious relic if you know what I mean."

"It should be in the Smithsonian. The gown that stopped armies and yours truly."

"Maybe I should get married in it."

"Not on your life! If we get married you're going to be properly respectable. It won't be a hippie wedding, you dope."

David's life was moving at a much faster clip than he'd anticipated. Despite his misgivings, he'd become somewhat involved in Pat's business, at first attracted to the computers there. He'd ended up taking computer courses at the nearby junior college, becoming the resident household computer genius. Pat had sighed a sigh of relief—her former husband had purchased and set up the machines before their divorce and her employees knew more about them than she did.

David's slack time decreased. The get-togethers with Harvey and Margaret became farther and farther apart, postponed, a chore. David realized with a start one day that he hadn't dressed as a woman for an entire month, and more than that, hadn't missed it. He couldn't say that he was truly happy, but he could say that he wasn't lonely and at loose ends any more. Parts of him wrangled and tangled with his decreased freedom.

On a camping trip that summer he didn't shave and upon returning—to the accompaniment of Pat's jokes—kept his mustache and let it grow bushy. At work, his boss and Gene Gatzo noticed with interest.

Sunlight streamed in the kitchen on a Sunday morning as Pat brought fresh-buttered English muffins to the table where David and Danielle sat. Both were playing their game of acting in TV commercials.

"Mmmm good. This is sooooooooooo good I could eat a thousand of them," said David as he put a generous helping of strawberry preserves on Dannie's muffins, then on Pat's and his own.

"You guys just can't get enough, can you?" Pat scolded. "You guys are going to get fat just like me."

"You, fat?" said David incredulously. "The way you work? No way, lady."

"No way, wade-y," chimed in Danielle. She wolfed down her muffin before the adults were halfway through and clamored for more.

"David, I've been thinking."

"Oh-oh."

"Why don't you quit work at the VA?"

"I'd love to. But I don't have an alternative."

"Are you kidding? With your stock photography and the computer work you're certainly doing your share here if that's what you're worried about."

He paused before replying. "I'll admit that I'd really love to go in and tell those SOBs off. Sorry about the bad language, Danny—tell 'em I don't need 'em, I mean."

"Go do it."

"I'll think about it. I mean, I have to think about losing my benefits and health plan and all that, too."

"Hi," said David as he flopped himself down next to Vince Grasso's neat desk. Vince looked up, surprised. They'd had very little contact lately. Office gossip had it that David was now living with someone respectable, not with someone like Corky. One thing hadn't changed, though—he was still habitually late.

"Can I help you?"

"I'm sick."

"You need to go home?"

"I mean, I'm sick of this place."

"Well, we all get sick of work at times. If you're stressed out or something, why don't you just fill out a sick leave slip and take the day off?" Vince adopted a soothing tone.

David started laughing as he looked away.

Vince shuffled some papers. "I think you'd better get back to your desk. I don't know who put you up to this but the joke's over."

"Really, I'm here to tell you that I'm quitting, resigning, whatever you call it. I'm giving a month's notice."

"Oh, surprise. I see. Well, I suppose it's nice when you can do that. What are you going to do, if you don't mind my asking?"

"Odds and ends. Odds and ends. I've got some things cooking."

"Well, I'm sorry to hear that you're leaving. You've been a valuable part of the team here."

"I've been a scalawag and you know it."

"Oh, well, we all have our off times. But I'd like to think that we were friends on the job here. You contributed a little variety to the office." Vince smiled knowingly. "Anyway, David, that's your final word, then? If you change your mind, you let me know right away, OK?"

As David walked to his cubicle, Vince wondered if his records clerk was going to be photographing weirdos full time.

"David, love, it's time we had our discussion about you

know what," said Pat, sitting on the sofa in the adjoining room as David finished washing dishes one evening. Danielle, tired after a long day of play, was fast asleep.

"Oh, yeah."

"'Oh, yeah,' is that all you can say? If I remember correctly, there was this small matter of marriage we were going to talk about."

David walked out to see her, wiping his hands on a dish-cloth. "Wait a minute. I have to go put on a pair of panties to get in the mood."

Pat ran over and grabbed him and he allowed her to force him to the living room carpet. "You're not getting away from me even though you're probably two-timing me and doing all kinds of things I don't know about," she chortled.

She got that way sometimes and he didn't always like that part of her. He wrestled himself to the top—he wasn't going to do any negotiating at the bottom of a pile—and pressed his body hard against hers. "So," he said gruffly, kissing her hard more out of self-defense than anything else, "will you marry me and make me king of the castle and give me half-interest in everything?"

"King, huh? Just where do I fit in? Yeah, that's probably exactly what you're thinking."

"Let's sit down on this, OK?" reasoned David. "I mean, look, what I want you to know is that I love you a lot and that you're the most important thing in the world to me now."

"Now?" She cocked her head to one side. "What about tomorrow and a year from now?"

David put his finger to his mouth and shushed her, then sat her down and poured petite glasses of amaretto. They set a date in November.

David lay in bed wearing the red Frederick's corset Pat had given him. He was alone in the house. Wondering what he could fantasize about, his mind raced about tapping that old memory, this fresh one. He fixed on Diane Beckelmeyer for a moment and resurrected the image of her whipping him with his hands tied. She would have an evil grin and she'd tease him, rubbing her breasts against his body.

Then he remembered various women he'd seen in ads—the

way the cups of their bras or corsets held their breasts and created smooth lines. He remembered the black bra Pat wore sometimes, the way the tight straps made small creases in the skin of her shoulder and back, and the way he photographed her wearing that bra. He could reach over to her chest of drawers and put it on if he wished. No, he was too close to coming. The sweetness was too great. Then he thought about the simpleness of her cunt, the rose-like flesh that had repulsed him the first time he'd seen it as a college student. Folds of wet skin upon folds of wet skin—Pat's ultimate softness. He had a full image of her cunt and amazingly it was propelling him to orgasm.

Never before had he managed an orgasm centered on a woman's cunt. Now he understood why women in porno magazines often exposed their cunts—guys got off on the rosy skin alone.

He was only too happy to leave the wedding details to Pat. He figured that if so many men had gone through the ceremony without screwing up too badly, then he could too.

Dear David,

We're so happy for you both and so anxious to meet Pat and see you again. Of course we can come out for the wedding.

We're wondering if you need any help financially. We're willing to help out if need be.

You haven't told us very much about Pat. We're in the dark!

Mother

I'm glad to see your life on track again. It makes us very happy. We were worried about you for a while there. We're glad that everything seems to be going good for you now. We're anxious to meet Pat.

Dad

Sometimes he asked himself if he was doing the right thing. He had set this whole program into motion without ever having a master plan for his life. "I mean," he wrote in his diary, "here I am getting married. How the hell did I ever get to this point? Am I trapped? Is this what I really want? It's too late to back out now — the champagne's been ordered."

Otherwise, their life seemed charmed while they prepared for November. They would soon be an official family — husband and wife and daughter — and everyone would think of them as such. Even their neighbors on Marwood Court would see the name on their mailbox — *The Nunleys* — and think that normalcy had returned. He and Patricia would get old together and have children and grandchildren. David, gray-haired, would be out raking leaves while she knitted on the porch.

20

It had rained earlier in the day, David could tell as he drove a rented car into the outskirts of Newsome, Ohio an hour after dark. His home town was deliciously familiar, yet there had been minor changes by those who had no respect for his memories. Where the road into town left the main highway the gas station had changed brands and there was a brash new burger stand. It had been much, much too long since he'd been back. Pat lay asleep on the seat beside him. The summer air was alive with the moisture of pervasive greenery and farmers' fields. Insects floated lazily around streetlights.

After David checked into the town's only motel and left Pat sleeping on a bed, he walked the rest of the way into town with a great sense of importance. He saw the field where he'd flown kites and fought mock wars as a kid, and a vast lawn where he'd played touch football. He watched entranced as fireflies cruised the darkness, winking at each other with tiny lanterns. Inside homes, the flickering glow of television sets confirmed that there really were people living here, just like in California.

With trepidation, he turned and began to walk up the street he grew up on—the street where his parents still lived. It was like entering the Navajo reservation again. He finally caught sight of the house where he grew up, dark and lifeless, and much smaller than he remembered. He wondered where his parents were, and remembered his mother on the phone a week before, inviting them out— "We'd like to buy your plane tickets." David remembered conspiring with Patricia to fly out unannounced a day early so they could check out the area before having to honor family obligations.

He slowly walked on the sidewalk in front of the house with all its gingerbread and history. The little trees planted when he was a boy were now as high as the second story. He didn't pause long because the town police car drove by on an adjacent street. David instinctively checked himself to see if he was in drag.

He walked further up the street under darkened, spreading elms, passing houses whose lawns he'd mowed as a boy. Memories of summers growing up flooded him—the sunny, sinful days of lying in deep green grass and fishing in little streams and going on expeditions with BB guns. His memory also dredged up winters of lying in his upstairs bedroom with windows made opaque by heavy frost. That cold, spartan room had almost driven him crazy with its repetitive-patterned wallpaper. He remembered hearing through his heating vent the sounds of his father powerfully shoveling coal into the basement furnace before going to bed. Through that same vent came the sounds of his parents fiercely arguing downstairs the next morning, and his mother's tears after the old man went to work.

At the far end of the street the public school stood on a hill in moonlight. In place of the old brick grade school was a modern glass and aluminum box. Next to the now-tamed stream where he and his buddies used to probe with sticks for crawfish was a new, trendy blacktopped playground. *Why can't my past remain the same? Why do things get covered over and forgotten?*

He forced himself to keep walking. People were probably watching, he thought, wondering what he was up to. Eventually he reached the small downtown and it was without life. He bumped into one semi-inebriated man who remembered him from school days and who invited him into Arnie's Bar but David politely declined.

As he walked under the big clock of the bank on the corner, he realized with a pang that his classmates here had already lived out a hundred stories of success or mediocrity while he played out his little transvestite drama in California. Many of them already had children and were running businesses.

David went on up to his old Methodist church in the north end of town. He loved the homely designs of the bricks in the walls, the white wooden steps and the illuminated steeple that went up to the stars. It was in this building that David had developed a crush on a just-married, very pretty woman in the choir and had once walked through her clothesline just to brush by her bras and panties.

Arriving back at his parents' house for a final reconnoiter before returning to the motel, there was still no sign of anyone. He walked up the long dark driveway to the patio at the rear of the house and sat in a metal lawn chair. Were his parents staying with one of his sisters overnight?

He rocked from side to side on the uneven legs of the chair until he remembered how as a kid he'd obsessively rocked himself in rocking chairs to anesthetize himself. And how he'd rolled in bed, like rolling halfway buried in sand, until his parents shouted at him to stop.

Finally resigning himself to return to the motel, he went to the back door of the house and turned the old ornate doorknob. To his surprise, the door opened. *Amazing – they still leave their doors unlocked around here.*

He went in and prowled around the house. Weak shafts of streetlight and moonlight penetrated the darkness and highlighted certain familiar scenes in an eerie fashion. He went in to use the bathroom and didn't turn the light on so as to preserve the mysteriousness. Not finding the toilet, he had fun peeing in the sink before moving on.

He heard the faint sound of a car. Its faraway sound brought him a deep loneliness, a loneliness he relished.

David wondered if Patricia out at the motel had awakened in an unfamiliar room and had forgotten that he'd left for a walk.

He gingerly began walking up creaking stairs to the upper floor of the house. Through lace curtains hung over a window he could see darkened neighbors' homes. Everything including himself seemed deliciously frozen in time.

He reached the top of the stairs and peeked in his old bedroom, lit gently by a nightlight. New wallpaper, same old bed. Then he walked stealthily down the hallway to his parents' room, the only bedroom being used. Their bed didn't seem as substantial and imposing as before. In fact, it seemed quite ordinary. His old Pandora's Box of sensual delights, his parents' chest of drawers, stood familiarly against a wall.

He flopped down on his parents' bed and let its coolness and firmness support him as he lightly began drifting off to sleep.

Unaware of how much time had passed, he jolted awake when he heard the crunch of automobile tires on the gravel driveway outside. He immediately reverted to a fifteen-year-old dressed in his mother's clothes masturbating on her bed while the rest of the family was at church. He involuntarily checked himself to see if he was wearing a bra.

How long am I going to be a frightened boy? How long will these charades go on?

He walked downstairs switching on lights as he went.

21

He did two things before the wedding, besides the expected.

He visited Diane one last time, and they traded stories about their lovers. Her photography was beginning to pay the bills. Afterward, they had quick straight sex, something they hadn't done since the first time on the couch. It seemed almost healthy.

Finally, two days before the wedding, he went into the woods around Crystal Springs Reservoir above San Mateo to camp overnight. He had always wanted to, even though he knew the San Francisco Water Department patrolled that area. Pat dropped him off so there would be no parked car to raise suspicions. He hiked a mile into the preserve in the late afternoon with a sleeping bag and the bare essentials, figuring this would be the Indian way of doing things. At any rate, it made more sense than a bachelor party.

He lay out his gear not far from the edge of the reservoir, hidden by trees from any observer. Soon darkness settled lightly over the valley. He lay on his sleeping bag wondering if the water department had secret ways of locating intruders. Maybe they used heat-sensing scopes. Then he began to think about his marriage. Suddenly it occurred to him, in a quick sweat, that, yes, he was getting married. Before, it had been more of a conception, an abstract thought. Now its enormity, a proximity he could taste, was brought home.

Just what am I getting myself into? I never really thought this through. What if I need to escape? What if I don't want to be a dutiful daddy all the time? Maybe Pat wants to erase all traces of Natalie. Maybe she's artfully been playing along just to snare me.

Maybe she really does love me. Maybe I'm the damned luckiest guy in the world.

He woke up numerous times during the night on the hard, uneven ground. During one such interlude he was looking at stars when out of nowhere an object streaked across the sky in a dazzling blaze of fire. It had grown distinctly brighter toward the end of its path when it simply disappeared in the air—no sound, no puff of smoke, no nothing. Pffffffffffft. A delicate star-tapestry had suddenly transformed into something highly potent and magical. David wondered why it had happened just then, and to him alone.

When he woke again, it was with a start. His heart was pounding and he had an overwhelming sense of everything ponderously closing in. Even his lungs seemed caught in a vise. He sucked in air ravenously as though each breath might be his last and thrashed around trying to get out of the sleeping bag. Finally able to control himself enough to unzip the bag, he sat taking in huge breaths of air. Everything around him seemed tinged with menace. The dark leaves of trees looked like spears. The earth itself seemed to be the wicked, dirty hide of a monstrous animal.

With time, his breathing and heart settled down, but he still couldn't spit out the pool of mad electricity inside him. There he was getting cold, sitting in his underwear—what if the Water Department found him this way! So he put on his trousers, sweater, and shoes without socks and began to walk in a big circle as though daring the menace to attack him.

When Pat picked him up hours later he decided not to tell her. It would only make her upset. David had decided the episode was similar to his fears about being drafted and going through Army boot camp. All that worry and sleeplessness about being ground into hamburger—and some of the fears had been justified.

That evening Pat and Danielle left for her bridal shower. David, unaccustomed to being alone in the house after work, warmed up some leftovers and sat down to watch TV. He still felt a psychic hangover from the previous night at the reservoir.

After watching some sexy lipstick and perfume commercials, he played with the idea of dressing as a woman again, mustache or not. It would make him feel more together. The delicious application of lingerie and a clinging red dress took his mind off his worries. Finally he had to decide whether or not to put on makeup.

So silly to dress up and try to look the part with a mustache. With misgivings, he painfully chopped away at his facial hair with a razor. There they went down the drain, those thick stubble hairs of manhood, and on went oily and fragrant substances from Pat's little cosmetic bottles. He was Natalie again.

She poured herself a glass of Zinfandel and sat down to watch more TV. In the privacy of the softly-lit room she played with herself absentmindedly and wondered if she should have an orgasm or wait until Pat came home to do something. Her indecision gave her a sour feeling.

She deliberated on the edge of tiredness for a half hour. Then she mocked herself. She'd shaved off her goddamn mustache for Christ's sake! She realized just how nice it was to have an appearance of guyhood. Still, she wondered if she could stand being David Nunley in thick Levi's and heavy men's shoes playing hubby for the rest of her life.

Why am I putting this trip on myself? Pat doesn't mind if I dress up, even after we're married. It's all inside me.

She went into the bathroom where Pat's makeup still sat on the shelf below the mirror and looked at herself. Natalie appeared genuine and ordinary.

God, it's good being Natalie again. She fits like a fine old glove.

She impulsively reached out, took one of Pat's lipsticks and dashed on the mirror—

Natalie and David
David and Natalie
You <u>are</u> such a pair!

In the reception line after the wedding ceremony, David stood next to Pat and his parents. They obviously loved his wife and thought he'd chosen well.

As the congenial line of guests gradually changed from close friends to distant relatives, David remembered briefly his parents' house in Ohio and walking downstairs to meet them.

They had come in the back door as they always did, his mother before his father. She had seen him first.

"David! David! We wondered who was turning on the lights. What a surprise!"

"We came early," he said, an unsure smile on his lips. "I wanted to show Pat the town but she conked out on me—she's out at the motel." He wanted to hug his mother as was their custom, but held back. She stood expectantly, holding her breath.

"Excuse me," his father said in a strained voice, conveniently leaving to go outside to feed the dog. His mother cocked her head to one side and smiled a smile of unabashed happiness and then the two of them came together in a great hug. David patted her back. She was older now, her hair thinner, but that smile was still the same.

"It feels good to be here."

She stepped back. "You're so good-looking in all those nice clothes."

"Pat helped me pick them out."

"I'm sorry, we went to a movie. If we'd only known you were already in town . . . What can I get you? You must be hungry."

"Well, I haven't had a Coke float in years."

His father came in finally as his mother was pouring Coke carefully over scoops of ice cream. Something about him seemed eager and playful, like the young man in David's dreams. "You didn't bring any of your dresses along, did you?"

"Now, Dad," bristled David's mother.

David instantly wanted to retaliate. His hope that they could talk about *it* in a sanitized way was quickly evaporating. "Why, do you want to see what I look like?"

"Not really. Do you still do it?"

David was off his strategy completely. "Ahhh, sure. It'll always be part of me."

"We think that probably your being married will have some effect," his mother said. The three of them were sitting around the kitchen table.

"It's true that since I met Pat my life has changed a bit. But she accepts that part of me."

"You know, David," his mother said, "I was remembering your teenage days, your high school days, and I was thinking—"

"I'd like to hear." He trusted her more than Maria Osaki.

"Well, what I remember is how unhappy you were with yourself at times. I don't know if it was us or what. I know I certainly felt inadequate in dealing with your moods. It seemed like you wanted to be someone else. Some days it was like dealing with a different person."

David considered the thought. "I remember I had an idea that if I put my mind to it I could make myself into anything I wanted to be. I needed some sort of formula—that's why I read all those psychology books."

His mother continued while his father seemed defused and almost gentle. "Maybe this was what led you into being a transvest—"

"Transvestite."

"Transvestite. That somehow you weren't happy so you tried to become another person."

David hadn't seen himself from quite that angle before. *Yeah, and I couldn't be a man because Dad was always stepping on me.* "It's true, I was going through a lot."

"Everyone, every guy, goes through a lot growing up," said his father, "but you sure took an unusual route."

David knew his father had said exactly the same thing to his mother a week or two before. Dad liked to repeat his thoughts.

"Well, Dad, can you accept me as I am?"

"I guess we can live with it. We don't want you to stay apart from us any more." There was a tear in his eye as he attempted an honest smile.

David, for once without thinking, went over and hugged him. His father at first was stiff. It was the first time they'd ever hugged. *I'm not afraid of him any more. He actually seems decent. What the hell will I do now?*

Snapping out of his mental fog and returning to the guests at his wedding reception, David looked over at his father. Dad was so much older now and more human. Being married to David's mother had changed him over the years. He was now a figurehead, and the torch was being passed to David, as reluctant as he was to carry it.

Pat lay against David's shoulder as they drove with windows down through the long open spaces of the Sacramento Valley at night. Lonely lights in the distance slowly blinked on and off. He struggled to keep the speed of the Volvo down.

"Well, David, how does it feel?"

"Christ. More responsible. Like a fucking adult. No kidding, I kind of enjoyed playing the role."

"You looked great in the tux."

"I didn't have time to really tell you this, but when you came down the isle you lit up the church with your smile. I'm not exaggerating. You looked so beautiful. Everyone said the same thing."

"I felt beautiful. It all just came together perfectly. Everyone got along so well."

David remembered the eclectic mix — his parents and brothers and sisters, Doctor Karen Vitriano and male friend, Harvey and Margaret, Diane and Laura with their children, the somber Gene Gatzo and girlfriend (and no duffel bag), Mrs. Johnson and her Polaroid camera, Jeanette, some of Pat's employees and distant Wyoming relatives, and several members of the Diana Society.

Pat reached down in the glow of the instrument panel, pulled his zipper open and reached inside. "I knew you'd be wearing these."

At midnight they pulled into the parking lot of a Lake Tahoe condo complex. Compared to the cold mountain air outside, the cozy apartment was soon warm with a blaze in the fireplace. After some microwaved food and leftover champagne, they went directly and immediately to bed.

They were awakened late the next morning by shafts of sunlight illuminating high white walls. "Well, aren't we supposed to be having a merry old orgy now?" he asked.

"Just supposed to be having fun," she said lazily.

He slithered over next to her, buried his face in her fragrant hair and put his leg between hers.

"So soon? It's too early."

"I'm a morning person, you know."

"Why don't you dress up? Now that you dropped your mustache you could look pretty convincing. Then make some breakfast and bring it to me in bed."

"You never did say anything much about the mustache thing."

"I figured it was your trip. I like you with it, like you without it."

"I don't know. I thought maybe I was outgrowing dressing up for a while there. Then remember what I wrote on the mirror?"

"Yes."

"I hadn't dressed for awhile. Then it felt so good being Natalie again. Like she wasn't a big production. It's hard to explain, but it's like she was really me."

"I hope you're not talking about having a sex change."

"Don't think so! But she was so down-to-earth. I mean, it was like I wasn't creating another person, I was creating the female me, someone who'd be the same a month or a year from now."

"I liked the way you looked that night. We had such a good romp. But, I'll tell you, I'm still worried about you wanting to become a woman full-time. I don't think I'd like that."

"So you wouldn't want me dressing as a woman all the time in the house, even if I still had a cock?"

"Hmmm. No. Besides, you couldn't be Natalie there all the time, anyway. You have to take showers, you have to shave, and we have guests over who don't know about Natalie."

"I was just testing you," David admitted. "There'll be a right time to do Natalie. Gee, maybe I should pick a new name. What fits this new image? Maybe more of a Swedish or Slavic name. I'll have to cast around." With that, he went whistling into the kitchenette to make some breakfast.

When he emerged a half-hour later, Pat had fallen back asleep, but the clatter of plates on a tray awakened her. Her eyes took a moment to adjust to the bright light, then she saw . . . a flat-chested and unshaven David dressed in a slinky nightgown with hairy legs ending in sneakers—and a big smile. "The new me," he announced. "Gender-fucker!"

"Oh my," postured Pat, "you really *do* need a new name. How about Man of all Seasons, Man for all Reasons. From Winter to Summer, Love's quite a number."

"I like that. Didn't know you were a poet."

"There's a lot you don't know about me."

"Just don't say you were ever a part-time hooker."

"What?"

"I'll have to tell you about Corky sometime. She was my Winter."

"Icicles?"

"Yeah. But now it's summertime. We're going to have a great, long summer, with fireflies and warm nights laying naked in bed."

"And tea and croissants every morning. I love you, David . . . *Dave*." She broke up laughing.

"And I love you, *Pattycakes*."

*T*he *Tri-X Chronicles* is a photographic book* documenting memorable events of the 1960s. In a surrealistic manner the book covers such events as the Viet Nam war, San Francisco love-ins, student strikes and unrest, and the battle over Berkeley's People's Park. In a section titled *Affairs*, the book offers more personal glimpses of people of the period.

To order within the United States, send $6.95 (money order or check) to *Alchemist/Light Publishing, Post Office Box 1275, Belmont, CA 94002*. The price includes mailing. Each additional book is $4.45. Orders to Canada and Mexico, $9.95 (postpaid) and to other countries (airmail delivery), $12.95 (make payment in U.S. dollars).

The Tri-X Chronicles includes some nudity and is for sale only to those over 18 years of age.

8-1/2 x 11" horizontal format paperback, black and white, 60 pages, printed by Tea Lautrec Co. of San Francisco, famed printer of many psychedelic/rock posters of the period.

bil paul   KD6JUI
1300 Pembroke Way
Dixon CA 95620
USA